the dangerous art of blending in

the dangerous art of  blending in

in

a novel by

ANGELO SURMELIS

BALZER + BRAY
An Imprint of HarperCollinsPublishers

Balzer + Bray is an imprint of HarperCollins Publishers.

The Dangerous Art of Blending In

ISBN 978-0-06-265900-2

Typography by Michelle Cunningham
17 18 19 20 21 PC/LSCH 10 9 8 7 6 5 4 3 2 1

First Edition

For Jennifer, Ed, and Judy

the
dangerous
art of
blending
in

one

I should've guessed something was up when I was walking home. There were cars parked all down my street. My mother's Bible study group is usually on Wednesday. Today is Tuesday.

I walk up to my house and open the door very quietly. "May the devil of lust and disobedience be cast out of his sinful shell."

My mother is in the living room with a circle of people from her church and Pastor Kiriaditis. There are candles flickering around them and they're praying together. I can see a framed photo of me in the center of the circle, on the coffee table. Luckily, they haven't seen me.

"We cast the devil's stronghold from his body. We pray to God for His mercy on his dark soul. Amen."

Where's Dad? Why is he never home when this shit goes down?

I start to hear more regular conversations, which indicates they are winding down.

"How can I thank you, Pastor?" I hear my mother saying. "I can't thank you enough for helping me. Let's pray he can stay in God's grace. He's a disobedient child."

I close my eyes and will myself to be calm. I quietly walk down the hall to my room but continue to listen. I hear my mother thank everyone again and usher them to the dining room for some spinach pie and Greek pastries. Nothing stops our family from eating.

I slip into my room. Here, surrounded by my things, I feel safe. With the wallpaper that I personally installed, and the wooden chair rail I put up during the holidays last year, I tried to give my boxy, tract-home bedroom some character. I wanted it to look like an old English library.

But all this just serves as evidence to my family that I'm a weirdo. None of it makes sense to them. "Why can't you have those sports pictures on your walls, like other boys?" Which is hilariously ironic because no one in my family is into any kinds of sports, except when Greece plays in the World Cup, or when the Greek team walks into a stadium during the Summer Olympic Games opening ceremonies. That's pretty much it. I'm literally the only one who is remotely interested in physical activity that does not include baking or going to work, the two forms of exercise that my family holds in high regard.

So back to my room. I've squeezed as many bookcases in this tiny space as possible. Being surrounded by books and magazines makes me feel calm. It makes the room seem wrapped in a layer of protection. As if nothing or no one can get to me.

Looking around, I think, *I need to talk to Henry*. He always calms me down, though after what I just saw, I should probably lay low. I scan the room. I can tell that someone has been going through my things.

My heart stops.

I glance over at my dresser, which is against the one wall that doesn't have any bookcases. Above it I installed shelving to store my art supplies. My once perfectly arranged boxes—the ones on top of the dresser, the ones holding the ticket stubs of every movie I've ever gone to—are all messed up. A box is open and some of the stubs are scattered on the dresser. I always put everything back where it belongs. But my mother was obviously looking for something. She assumes most of the time that I must hide drugs in my room.

Watching movies or TV shows that are about God, Jesus, or some kind of spiritual journey or lesson are approved. All other forms of entertainment are "the work of the devil, narcissistic, selfish, and only for girls and the gays."

I open the drawer where I keep my notebook. It's below a pile of neatly stacked books. I quickly leaf through it. All the pages are still there. I exhale but I tell myself I really should have hidden my notebook in a much better place. I should have buried it with the others outside the house. It's been a while since she's been on a search-and-destroy mission. I've become too complacent. Was that the reason for today's meeting? I pull my phone out of my pocket and stare at it. I want to text Henry. I put it back in my pocket and crawl into bed. I intend to lie there just for a bit, but I'm exhausted.

I fall asleep hard.

two

"*Evan*. Evan."

My dad is bent over me.

I squint at him. "What time is it?"

"It's almost five."

"In the morning?"

He looks at me strangely. "Yeah. Do you want to go get doughnuts?" He stands up straight. This is a thing my dad and I do. He usually gets up at four a.m. and is out the door no later than five. His work at the bakery starts early, and on certain days, he wakes me up and we go to Dunkin' Donuts. Ironic that we go to a doughnut chain when his work, his life, is baking. We sit at the counter. He orders coffee and a doughnut. I order a doughnut, sometimes two, and we mostly sit there in silence. If he's feeling like we have some extra money that month, he buys a dozen on our way out. Then he takes me back home and goes to work.

I get up and look for my shoes. I fell asleep with my clothes on. I check my phone. It's a bunch of texts from Henry after I dozed off.

Where RU?

Home?

Just drove by house. WTF, is there a party?

Call. CU

I should have texted him. I run to the bathroom and turn on the faucet, but not full blast so that I don't wake my mother. I splash some water on my face and try to tame my hair with my wet hands. It's not working. I sneak back to my room, grab a baseball cap, and meet my dad outside. He's got the car already running and is leaning against the trunk taking long drags off his Marlboro Light. He's looking toward the house across the street. With the streetlight hitting his face, his already strong profile is even more prominent. My dad has the kind of looks I wish I'd inherited. His face is bold, with angular features and a sharp, severe nose. My face looks like my mother's.

He hears me opening the passenger door and comes around to the driver's side. A cigarette dangles from his mouth as he slowly closes the door. He doesn't want to wake her either.

"I can go in a little later today. Want to try a different Dunkin' Donuts?"

Our neighborhood Dunkin' is less than a mile away. We could walk there, if we really wanted to.

"Sure. Which one?"

"I don't know. I saw one the other day on the way home. It's in the opposite direction of the one we usually go to. It looked bigger."

Bigger is code for better. More is also better. *Bigger* and *more* are not things my family can afford, so when there's an opportunity to partake in one or the other—or, on that rarest of occasions, both—we're all in.

The window on my dad's side of the car is halfway down. He holds his cigarette out of it when he's not smoking. He knows that cigarette smoke makes me dizzy, but I never have the heart to tell him that when he does that—open the window—the air actually just blows the smoke back and straight into my face. Usually most of my time in the car with him is spent trying to find new ways to hold my breath. But I don't mind because we're spending time together. A little secondhand smoke and light-headedness is a small price to pay.

The ride is in silence. We're on surface roads. This time of day is kind of perfect. It's so still. I actually let myself wonder if this could be the start of something new and better.

I daydream that maybe, suddenly, everything in Kalakee, Illinois, starts to change. My hair goes straight and floppy. The flat landscape is suddenly circled by lush, flowering hills. I can walk into any room filled with people without sweating. Everywhere. No more Greek school on the weekends. Our house is quiet and safe and I am loved.

"We're here."

My dad tosses a cigarette out the window.

I get out of the car and follow him inside. The place is almost empty except for two guys, both hunched over at the end of the counter, sitting side by side. Their heads are buried in the *Chicago Tribune.*

"Good morning, Eli." The waitress behind the counter has a big, friendly smile.

Obviously my dad has been to this Dunkin' without me.

We sit down at the counter.

"Is this your son?" She places a coffee cup in front of my dad with one hand and effortlessly pours with the other.

"Yes. This is Evan. For Evangelos, but he likes Evan." He taps me on the head as if I'm five years old.

I smile at her. She has a broad, open, and friendly face.

"Handsome must run in the family." The words lilt from her mouth as she searches for a coffee cup for me. "My name's Linda. For Linda."

My dad says, "He's not drinking coffee."

"Nice to meet you, Linda." I do want coffee. I want a lot of coffee.

Linda leans on the counter, her hands spread apart. She looks at both of us and asks, "What do you gentlemen want this morning?"

"I'll have a cruller and Evan will do a chocolate glazed." My dad looks at me just to make sure.

That's pretty much my standing order. I've been known

to eat at least half a dozen of them in one sitting. You'd think I'd be larger, but my theory is that the internal nervous energy I work so hard to conceal keeps my metabolism running on high.

Linda is off to get the doughnuts. My dad is drinking his coffee and staring at the doughnut racks in front of us.

"Did you sleep okay?" he wants to know.

"Fine."

I don't mention the nightmares. My dad means well, but he doesn't want to hear about things like nightmares. He wants to hear things like "I slept fine."

"We didn't wake you for dinner last night because we assumed you were exhausted. You must be starving. What do you want to drink?" Before I can even answer, he motions toward Linda, "Hon, get the boy another doughnut, and he'll have a milk."

With this sugar rush, I am going to be on fire for the first few hours of class.

"Here you go, dears." Linda places our doughnuts and my milk on the counter and floats away.

"I heard about yesterday," my father says with a mouthful of cruller. He takes a swig of coffee and motions for a refill.

"What did you hear?"

"I heard some people from church came over."

Just as I'm about to take a bite of my chocolate glazed. The most important bite—the first one. The one that sets the tone for the rest of the doughnut experience.

I stop myself. Put the doughnut down and swivel to look at him. This is a very calculated move. I want him to know that the next thing I'm going to say is important.

"Dad, they think I have a demon inside me. Does that seem normal to you?"

"Oh, don't be so dramatic. They were just praying for you. Nothing wrong with that."

I ask him again. "Do you think I have demons?"

"Apparently not anymore." He's amused with himself.

I still haven't taken a bite of the doughnut. Does he not notice? No one loves doughnuts more than I do.

"This isn't funny. She's making it harder and harder for me to have any kind of normal life." When he doesn't say anything, I add, "And I have nightmares. I don't sleep fine."

"Evan. Eat."

I start in on it and say with a mouthful, "I'm not the one being dramatic. She's creating it. What happened was—*is*—"

"Evan." He looks right at me. "Let's drop this. It'll pass."

"It won't." Under my breath: "She always gets away with it." I'm mad at my father right now. Disappointed. It's easy to be angry with her, but I expect more from him.

"Your friend asked about you a lot when you were at Bible camp."

That's out of left field. "Henry?"

"He came by the house. I was outside working on the car."

"He knows we're not allowed phones or—"

"He just wanted to see how you were. If we had heard from you."

"I'll see him today."

He nods.

"Your mother thinks—*we* think—that Bible camp was a good change this year."

"I could have gone camping with Henry and his family in Wisconsin again this year."

"Maybe next year." He turns. "Linda, we'll take a dozen assorted to go. Make sure there are six chocolate glazed, three crullers, and Evan will pick the rest." My father takes out a big wad of cash from his front pocket and hands it to me. "Pay the lady. I'll be outside."

"What's with all the cash?"

"I went to the bank yesterday. We're not using credit cards right now. Emergencies only."

He goes out, lights a cigarette, and leans up against the car. It's not autumn yet, though he's dressed for it. He's wearing a beige cable-knit turtleneck sweater and too-tight cords. It's an outfit that he can pull off, but it embarrasses me. I've had female teachers tell me how good-looking my father is, in a very inappropriate way.

"Here you go, Evan. I made the rest some of my favorites,

if that's okay with you." Linda hands me the box of doughnuts. "How old are you, honey?"

"Seventeen. I'll be eighteen in October. I plan on getting a car soon."

Why did I say that? Linda doesn't care about my transportation plans. The sugar is starting to take effect and I'm running all my words together.

"Do you have a girlfriend?" she asks with her big, broad smile. "You must. I bet she's really pretty."

I turn bright red, hand her the money, and walk out.

We're pulling out of the parking lot when I say to my dad, "Why do you put up with her?"

I regret the words even as they are coming out of my mouth. He never takes his eyes off the road.

"You know she's had a hard life. There's a lot you don't know. Your mother's childhood back in Greece wasn't easy."

My go-to move normally is to just nod my head and pretend to understand. But I don't understand. How can someone who had a difficult life want to make their child's life even harder?

"That's no reason to do what she does. I'm getting too big to beat, so now she punishes me with mind games and this prayer shit. I don't understand it."

"*Evan!*" His eyes are still on the road.

"I'm sorry."

I whisper, almost to myself, "Have you forgotten all the things she's done over the years?" *Have you forgotten my entire life?*

I can tell just by looking at his face that he hasn't.

I'm seven years old. Dad leaves the apartment at four a.m. for his first gig. He works all day at the bakery. He'll come home for a quick shower midafternoon, and then go off to the next job, as a restaurant line cook. Sometimes he doesn't get home till ten p.m.

Today when he came home between jobs, he found me in the corner of the living room. In a ball. Blood coming down my face from somewhere under my hair. It's summer with a lot of midwestern humidity. We don't have air-conditioning in the apartment, and the mixture of sweat and blood is such a weird, uncomfortable feeling. I'm too scared to get up and go anywhere else in the house.

He calls to me but I don't move. He walks over and places his hand on my head. He can feel the lumps. I know he can. At that moment, my mother walks into the living room from the bedroom. I hold my breath.

It would be better if he hadn't found me, because the fact that he has makes it into a "thing" with my mom. And once he leaves for his second shift, everything gets worse. He usually never says anything when this stuff happens. I want to believe that he secretly yells at her. But she's usually the one yelling at him.

Today is different.

He lifts his hand off my head. My left eye must be swollen shut. I can't see anything out of it. I turn slightly so I can see the action with my right eye. My shirt is drenched and sticking to my body. He walks toward her and grabs her upper left arm. I can tell the force of his grip on her bare skin by the way his fingers look—all red and white.

They just look at each other. She starts to cry.

Her crying no longer affects me. It stopped having an effect on me about a year ago.

He pulls her into their bedroom and closes the door behind them but I can hear clearly. It's a cheap apartment with even cheaper walls, windows, and doors.

"Are you trying to kill him? Is that what you want?"

I've never heard him speak this way to her.

"Do you want me to come home to a dead child?" His voice is escalating. She's sobbing.

He continues. "I don't know what to do here. I don't know what to do. I can't."

"He's not a good person. I don't want him. I want him gone." I can tell she believes it. I've heard it so many times that I believe it.

Am I bad?

Is there something wrong with me?

"This isn't right. It has to stop. One day he won't survive this and it'll be on you."

I can tell he's too tired to continue, but I don't want him to stop.

I want him to yell at her.

To hit her the way she hits me, beats me, throws things at me. But I know that will only make her stronger.

We pull up in front of the house. I stare down at my box of doughnuts and take off my baseball cap.

"Evan, just try. Please."

Isn't that what I've been doing for years?

I take a breath and look out the passenger window. "Why the credit card freeze?"

"Things are kind of tough right now. My hours are getting cut back. And this house. It takes a lot. Plus there's your Greek school to pay for."

"We didn't have to buy these doughnuts."

"Doughnuts aren't the problem." He reaches over and musses my already wild nest of hair.

"Dad." I duck my head away.

"It's okay—I didn't mess up your precious hair. It would be easier if we could afford to send you to the private church school. It's difficult straddling both worlds."

"I need a haircut. It looks ridiculous."

The thing he doesn't know: *I'm actually straddling multiple worlds.*

"I wish I had your hair. Look at this." He points to the sides of his head, where his hair is the thickest, and pulls his wavy strands out as much as he can. "I look like Larry from the Three Stooges."

My dad loves the Three Stooges. They're one of the few things that make him laugh out loud.

Inside the house, I place the box of doughnuts on the kitchen table and go downstairs to the small bathroom to take a shower. I don't want to wake her. She usually doesn't fall asleep till three, four, sometimes five a.m. She sleeps her hardest in the early morning. It's when I feel the safest. I want to get out and go to school before she's up.

I grab my backpack and open the drawer where I put my notebook. I stick it in my backpack and head out as quietly as possible.

three

Walking to school is one of the best parts of my day. I'm alone. I can dream all the way there, usually uninterrupted—totally at peace. Daydreaming is one of those things on my mom's Sin List or Lazy List. So I try to get it in when I can.

Until this summer, the dream in my head has been pretty much the same every time. Kind of basic, boring, completely unsexy stuff. If someone accidently stumbled into my fantasy life, they'd be seriously disappointed.

It consists of me living on my own, preferably in a big city. The bigger the better. My days are stress free. Normal. I have better hair. The kind of hair that I don't have to pay attention to. You know the guys who just wake up and go? I'd be one of those guys. Like Henry Kimball. We can play tennis for hours and I wind up looking like the offspring of the Bride of Frankenstein and Albert Einstein. Henry looks like—well, he looks like Henry.

I pull out my phone and start to text him:

Hey. Sorry I missed texts earlier. Walking 2school. CU later?

"Panos!"

It's Jeremy Ludecker. He's a last namer. He's running up behind me and I can hear him wheezing. I think it's his allergies.

"Panos! I know you can hear me, Pube Head. I'm running out of breath here. You know my asthma's a bitch."

Asthma, right. I get the two mixed up. I stop and look behind me. He runs right into me, knocking us both to the ground, landing on top of me. My phone is knocked out of my hand. He is wheezing straight into my face. I can smell bacon.

"Jeremy. Always a pleasure." I'm trying to pry him off me and find a way to not make the whole exchange look awkward. Failing miserably on both counts.

He springs up and holds out his hand. I ignore the hand and lift myself up, adjusting my backpack and going after my phone. Before I can say anything, he starts in.

"What was with all the cars in front of your house yesterday? I rode my bike past it to see if you wanted to go to the trails and there were cars everywhere. Your driveway was stupid. You weren't returning my texts and then I was going to knock, but I didn't want to have to deal with a bunch of people who didn't speak English. Are you seriously still the only one in your family who can communicate with the outside world? Because I have to—"

He's known forever that my parents demand we speak Greek at home, but he still has to be a jerk about it. "Jeremy, my parents had company over for dinner. Don't be a dick. You can't spell shit and we do it in two different languages. Did you go to the trails? Anything cool?" I look down at the phone. Nothing yet.

"Sorry, man. No trails."

The trails are old bike paths where there were once open fields. They go on forever. They start in our subdivision, which used to be nothing but farmland, and keep going. Most of the land is empty, with the occasional abandoned and in-shambles barn, but if you go for a while, like at least fifteen miles, the trails start to merge into existing working farms. The people who live and work there don't like us, or anyone, coming through. If you aren't careful, they'll shoot right at you.

I want to change the subject. I've become a bit of an expert at separating my worlds. I don't want them merging. Especially now.

"I went to your uncle's bowling alley instead," says Jeremy. "You know I can't pass up the awesomeness of free games."

I'm so uncomfortable with this arrangement. My uncle Tasos knows that Jeremy is my friend and he lets him bowl and play video games without having to pay. He even gives him free food. Besides my dad, my uncle is probably my favorite family member, maybe because Tasos married into it. The bowling alley he owns is attached to a full restaurant and dining hall.

Here's the thing: Jeremy knows I don't like him going there without me. Not because I always long for his company, but because it's not a good idea.

It's just not. Worlds colliding sort of thing.

"I told you not to go there without me."

"It's one of the perks of being your friend, Pubes. That and you doing my art class homework for me. Hey!"

"What?"

"Panos, what the fuck are you staring at that phone for?"

"Just waiting for a—"

"Fucking Kimball, right? It's always Kimball. Did you miss your boyfriend while you were at Camp Holy-Hole?" He snort-laughs at himself so hard his asthma kicks in.

"It's like you're aging backward. Idiot."

Still no text from Henry. What's he doing?

"If you two didn't spend so much time together, maybe you and I could actually get some shit done. How much tennis can two people play? It's the most boring sport."

We're almost at the school entrance, and Jeremy spots Tess Burgeon. He shouts in her direction, "Burge! I have a lollipop with your name on it. It's grape. You want it? I want to watch you lick it."

"What the fuck, dude?" He's all class, that Jeremy.

"I know she digs me. Jorgenson too, probably."

"Kris?"

"They're always hanging out together and I can feel the vibes."

I laugh. "You're delusional."

"There she is. You'll see." Jeremy cups his hands and yells. "Jorgenson!"

Kris sees him wave and starts heading this way. Oh, this should be good.

Jeremy turns back to me. "Wait for it."

"I will."

Kris has one of those faces that are difficult to read. It looks like she's in a good mood even when she's not smiling. Her light-brown eyes are set far apart and her hair is all big, natural curls right past her shoulders. A little blond and a lot of dark roots.

"What's up?" Kris asks as she approaches us. She's right next to Jeremy now and she's taller than he is, which in this moment I really appreciate.

Jeremy starts, "Let's be honest, Jorgenson. You and Burge are taken with me."

Without missing a beat, Kris nods. "Totally."

Jeremy smirks and raises an eyebrow at me.

"Go on," he says.

"Well, it's a classic problem. Two friends. One boy. Who will he choose? You know how it is."

I'm dying.

Jeremy puts his hand over his heart. "Kris, I'm not one to break hearts, but you know my love for the Burge."

Kris closes her eyes and takes a breath. "She's my friend and I want her to be happy. Go to her, Jeremy."

He puts his hand on her shoulder and says, "Jorgenson, don't miss me too much."

Then he turns to me before he bolts off. "I'll see you at lunch. Let's make plans for tonight. Oh, and some guy named Cage was at your uncle's. He was asking about you. What kind of name is Cage?"

"It's Gaige."

Shit.

What the hell is Gaige doing here?

Kris breaks into my panicked thoughts. "I know I'm kinda new here, but how is it that you two are friends?"

I laugh. "He's one of the first people I met when we moved here. Can't really shake him."

"I can see that. Much respect to you for putting up with him. Sometimes I really just want to punch him in the face," she says, but she's smiling.

"Oh, please don't. You'll break him. Actually, maybe you should. It would probably be good for him."

"Not a good idea. Got into trouble at my old school for all the wrong reasons."

"What, violence?" I'm half joking.

"I have a difficult time letting people get away with shit."

"Huh?"

She smiles again. "Rumors become fact real fast. See you later, Evan."

As I'm trying to piece together what she means, another thought strikes me. *What must it be like to feel so comfortable in your own skin?*

Our high school isn't spectacular, but it does have one thing that I love—an atrium. The school is basically a square with a hole in the middle, and in that hole is the atrium. Which means the literal heart of the school is this open-air garden. All the hallways have doors that lead out to the center.

This is where I go now. To get away from the Jeremys and my dad and my mother. And sometimes, myself. And now to get away from Gaige.

Who is apparently here.

Here in my town. Where I live. Where my parents live.

Mr. Overstreet, head janitor and gardener, is in there working on the plants. The door from the north hall is propped open with an enormous trash bin. I walk in, duck down, and make my way to the plantings on the west side, where there are tall grasses and plenty of Virginia bluebells in bloom. I lie underneath them and stare up at the clean, blue sky.

It's funny how you get so used to winter that you forget there are any other seasons.

I close my eyes.

I breathe.

The atrium was closed all last year. No one was allowed to go out into it because Lonny Cho, Scott Sullivan, and Gabe Jimenez were all caught there at night with a bunch of other kids from River Park High. The janitors found condoms and cigarette butts along with beer bottles. It was a huge deal. Bigger than it should have been, if you ask me. I mean, at least they were using condoms. The boys from our school were suspended and the atrium was off limits for a whole year.

I take out my notebook and turn to the first blank page. With a pen I begin to sketch this garden. Not exactly how it looks but how I see it in my mind. My phone buzzes. It's Henry.

Just saw. Running late 2day-talk after schl?

K

I continue drawing. The garden is wild and out of control. The plants and flowers grow higher than normal and at a certain level they start to intertwine—almost like they're forming bridges. Canopies. I stare at my sketch. *Rumors become fact real fast.* Hmmm. What if Gaige is here to expose me? My breathing starts to get short.

Maybe I want to be found out. Maybe it's time to have something real to be in trouble for.

No.

Not now.

· · ·

I'm heading to first period, which is English, and it's a decent class. Decent in the sense that I do my work with very little interruption. The teacher, Mrs. Lynwood, doesn't try too hard to connect with us and I can kind of go unnoticed. That's pretty much my goal in school. *To not stand out.*

I'm running a little late, so I cut through the cafeteria even though we're not supposed to during class hours. The cafeteria is empty except for Tommy Goliski, heading in the opposite direction.

Great.

Tommy is the guy you do not want noticing you unless you're in his crowd or a great athlete, which I am not. He has very little patience for anyone else.

I've spent my whole high school career cultivating an air of nothingness. I put my head down and keep walking.

"Evan Panos." He stops right in front of me.

I look up at him, and I must have the face of someone who's just been told they've been randomly chosen to sing the national anthem at a Cubs game. Like, "Hi, you in the back row of the bleachers. Yes, you, with the striped shirt and khaki shorts. Please come down and sing the national anthem in front of all these people!"

I have that face. Because how the hell does Tommy Goliski even know my name?

"I know you're late, but this is important. I want to help

you. Save you, actually."

I try to keep a neutral "listening" face, though I have no idea what he's talking about. Why is everyone trying to "save me"? Is Tommy going to perform some kind of dork-nerd exorcism?

"You know, you could be a cool kid. Maybe." He gives me a casual once-over. "The makings are there, I think, but you need some kind of personality. Probably some other stuff too." I continue to look at him blankly, which is totally proving his point. "I think I can help you. Help this." He points at me as if I'm a kind of food behind glass in the cafeteria that he wants to make adjustments to before he puts it on his tray.

What is happening?

"Do you want my help? Do you want to stop looking like a nobody?"

I don't know what to say to this.

"I'm going to be really late," I mumble.

"No one can figure you out. Are you smart? Dumb? Gay? Are you even interested in anything? Even your clothes are, they're just, I don't know. Nothing."

I stiffen.

He continues, "You're not gonna say anything?" I'm almost equal parts embarrassed and mad. More mad. "You know, it's not that you're ugly, exactly. It's that you're . . ." He steps back and shakes his head. "Fuck, the hair would be the first thing to go." He laughs and oddly—for a big guy—his voice squeaks.

He starts to walk toward the exit. "Also getting you to the gym. You're like a Twizzler. With stupid hair." Now he's all-out laughing, practically hunched over.

Asshole. I want to fight back, but I don't. I'm afraid of what I might do to him.

four

I slink into Mrs. Lynwood's class. Luckily I sit toward the back. Easy in, easy out. It's part of my no-identity identity. Tess Burgeon sits directly in front of me. The back of her head is so shiny. I mean her hair. It's perfectly straight and kind of mesmerizing. So golden and bright, with subtle hues of red.

I notice too much. Every little thing in a room about a person, place, anything, feels like it's giving off a signal, like everything is trying to communicate with me. That's why I love neat, well-organized rooms. There's less noise and my head feels calm.

"Miss Burgeon, can you hand the short stories back to everyone?" Mrs. Lynwood points to a stack on her desk. She always wants us to write on paper, with a black pen. It frustrates almost everyone in the class. They just want to write on their laptops and email her the finished product, but she insists on something we can all hold, mark on, and flip through. I don't mind it. I actually prefer it. It helps me focus to have a pen or pencil in my hand and write, draw, scribble something. Lately, since coming back from camp, it seems like all the stuff in my head is slowly drifting off, as if it's smoke escaping from a window and into the sky, far away, making room for things I want to put in there. I think I want new experiences. New memories, not the ones others have given me. Using a pencil and paper to mark, draw, write something different is another opportunity to give myself something new. Something good.

Mrs. Lynwood is standing behind her desk with her hands on her hips. Not in an *I'm about to let you kids in on some Lynwood wisdom* sort of way, but more disappointment.

Tess approaches my desk, places my short story on it, and whispers, "Tell your asshole friend to leave me alone."

I'm not totally surprised. Anyone can see why she'd say that. Jeremy can be a complete dick, but there's something good in there. I've seen it. I think he genuinely likes Tess and I thought she liked him back. She asks me about him all the time. "What did you and Jeremy do last night? Are you guys going to Lonny's party?" Could I have read the whole thing wrong?

Mrs. Lynwood says, "The lesson I want you to take away from these stories is that there is no right or wrong way to write them. But most of you took the approach of what you thought I *wanted* to see."

We all just look at her.

"So I am not going to grade them, because I don't think you

did the work you were meant to do. I'm giving you a chance to write your story again. You can take the rest of the week and this weekend. I'll collect them on Monday."

No one is happy about this, including me. I don't know when I'm going to have time to write something else. I'm working this weekend, our family is hosting a church luncheon on Sunday, and I have to register for Greek school, which I've been going to since I was seven.

Mostly, I'm scrambling to do different things to please different people. I wonder what would happen if I only spent time doing what interested me.

five

My mother is calling.

I let it go to voice mail.

There's no mistaking that my mom's not originally from Kalakee. Her accent is heavy. She's barely five foot one but claims to be five foot two. She has thick dark brown hair that rests just above her chin, worn in a tight curl. Her face is round. Broad and pretty with full lips, big black eyes, a generous nose, and perfectly arched eyebrows. Everything about her appearance is meticulous. The only makeup she wears is Walgreen's no-name-brand lipstick. Color: Nude.

Almost everyone who meets my mother thinks of her as pleasant. "Nice," even. She works hard to make you think she's easygoing, unless she really doesn't approve of you. Then it's difficult for her to disguise her disgust.

She works at Duane's Depot, not too far from our house. She can walk there. Her bright-blue smock that she has to wear is always perfectly pressed. The blue plastic Duane's nametag is on straight, and when she's arranging cans of vegetables on a shelf at the Depot, they're lined up with extreme precision.

My phone is showing one new message.

I walk over to my locker, open it, lean in, and listen. She's whispering in Greek, "Evan, don't forget to get your hair cut after school. We have church company this Sunday and you can't be looking like a lesbian. Do *not* spend that money I gave you on anything else but a haircut. Come by the store after so I can see it to make sure it looks good."

I press Delete.

six

At the end of every school day, I start to feel sick to my stomach. Just at the thought of going back home.

Henry walks up. "Hey!"

He falls into step with me. "Hi," I say.

"Finally. It's been a minute." His smile is big and his green eyes are staring into mine. When the sun hits them they seem impossibly light.

I haven't seen him since before camp. He looks different. Like he's still Henry but he's . . . oh shit . . . he's handsome. It's like all the pieces have clicked into place—he's grown into himself. His upper body looks fuller. And I'm trying to avoid looking at his full lips.

Shit. Stop it.

"What's with the face? I haven't seen you in forever and this is the face?"

"What the fuck are you talking about?" I'm concentrating

on making my face as bland as possible.

He has deep dimples that come out when he's smiling. The one on the right side seems like it's higher and deeper than the one on the left. *Why have I never noticed this before?* He's always been so goofy, especially since he's tall—six foot two. His T-shirt looks like it's straining against his muscles.

He brushes up on my shoulder and we are now heading away from campus. I have never been uncomfortable around him, but now my mouth is dry and my hands are sweating.

Luckily Henry doesn't seem to notice. "I texted you like four times yesterday. What were you up to? After school?"

Oh, the usual . . . trying not to set my mother off and avoiding you (which is the last thing I want) because I don't know what to say to you since Bible camp and . . . Gaige.

"Just homework and family stuff. You know. You? How was your summer?"

"All I did was tennis. Tennis in the morning. Afternoon. Night. Fuck. I practiced, worked out, swam. This fucking scholarship is turning into a full-time job."

"It's good, though, right?"

"I guess. It'll pay for most of college, but I don't know."

"What?"

"Ev, It's boring. I want to hear about you."

"It's the same over here too. See what happens when we don't hang out?"

"You're the dick who left. I had all kinds of plans for us."

"What?"

"Doesn't matter now. You left and I turned into a tennis zombie who roams the streets at night with a racket hungry for . . ." He stops himself, then starts laughing.

"What's going on?"

He tries to recover. "OMG, I was trying to make a zombie-tennis reference. *Hungry for—balls.*" He bursts out laughing again. "It's so dumb, I know. And yet . . ."

"So this is what happens when I leave you alone. You turn into Jeremy."

"Shut up!"

"C'mon. Pull yourself together and tell me about those awesome Kimball plans. You never plan."

"Oh, I plan shit. I plan the shit out of shit."

I start to laugh. "Such a lie."

"That stupid laugh. Ev, It's embarrassing. For you, I mean."

"Fuck you. You love it like a lover."

"*Ugh!* You know how much I hate that word."

"Speaking of your *lover*, how's Amanda?" I ask casually.

"She doesn't like to sweat." Then he gets more serious. "Also, we broke up."

Breathe, Evan.

"I'm sorry." I'm really not, though.

"Don't be. I'm good." He changes his tone. "C'mon. How was camp? Did you get more holy?"

"It was fine." I'm straining to act casual.

"What?"

"Nothing."

"Ev, you're all . . ."

"No. It was good. Just long. It was a long summer."

"We need to catch up. I have to practice this afternoon— you up for a set? Might as well play together before the weather turns."

"Can't. I have to get my hair cut, and then homework—"

"Get your hair cut another day. It looks good longer. Like old-school Taylor Swift. If Taylor Swift had brown hair and was a Greek boy."

"Uh, I'm not sure that's a compliment."

"Ev. C'mon. It's been a whole summer."

"I have to get it cut for work," I lie. My boss has no opinion on the length of my hair. "They don't like for you to have long hair in a deli."

"You got that job?"

"Yeah. It helped that I applied right before camp."

"Cool. Better that than a hair net. What about this week-end? Can we hang? Why am I begging? Not cool." He starts to head toward the bus. He doesn't live within walking distance. He's closer to the old monastery I found on one of my bike rides. I've never told him about it.

As he approaches the bus, he turns around and yells, "Ev, don't get it cut too short!"

I feel my face go tomato red. I find myself running a hand through my hair, imagining it through his eyes. When I realize what I'm doing, I immediately pull my hand away and start walking the other direction into town.

Getting a haircut is something I prefer to get over with as quickly as possible. Very little small talk and even less mirror gazing. I always dread when they turn you around in the chair to see the finished product. You have to look. Like really look. What are they hoping you'll see? It's not like I'm instantly turning into some awesome version of myself. It's me with shorter hair. But still me.

I walk past all the stores in town that I've walked by hundreds of times. Looking in the windows and creating stories about the people I see. I always imagine that everyone's life is better than mine. It has to be. I want it to be.

I cross the street when I come to Sandee's Hallmark store. I stole a jewelry box from there when I was eight. My mom wanted it for so long . . . went on and on about what it would mean to own *such a beautiful thing*. When she opened it on Christmas morning, she squealed and gushed and hugged and kissed me.

She was so happy.

It felt like all the broken pieces inside me gathered together and stayed put for that moment.

She never questioned how an eight-year-old could afford such a thing.

But for a few hours I felt like she loved me.

I still worry every time I pass Sandee's that I'll be found out.

The haircut isn't bad. Actually, it looks kind of good. I walk over to Duane's Depot with a confident stride. I think my mother might actually approve of this one.

Duane's Depot does not have the class of a Target or the cheapness of a Dollar Store. It's got a lot of the same type of merchandise, but not the style or the low price. I've never understood how it's still in business. Especially when there is an actual Target less than fifteen miles away.

I walk into the Depot and I'm instantly greeted by Patty. She's Duane's "Aunt Dilly," which is Duane-speak for store greeter. I don't see Patty often, but when I do it's always as if she's seeing me for the first time.

"Howdy, Evan! Here to see your mama? I love that woman. Never has a bad word for anyone. The other day, she made baklava for all of us here, and we could not even stand it, it was so moist, flaky, and scrumptious. You and your papa are lucky little men."

Patty is from the Midwest, born and bred, yet somehow she always speaks as if she grew up in a part of the South that no one has ever heard of. Like an actress doing the most over-the-top Southern accent ever.

My mother is a genius at making everyone who isn't in her immediate family fall in love with her. Unless she deems you "so evil" that she won't even pretend. No one would ever suspect her of anything awful. She could literally gut and slaughter a street full of people in this town, and no jury would believe this tiny, doe-eyed lady would ever be capable of such a thing.

"I'm here to see her. How are you, Patty?"

"I am plumb sweet right now. We've put those drinking glasses that have the painted oranges on them on deep discount. Now that summer is over we're featuring ones with acorns painted on them. Acorns! How cute, right? The orange ones are fifty cents! Did you hear that? Fifty cents!"

I am standing less than a foot away from her. There is no way for me to not hear her.

"That's awesome. Do you know where my mom is?"

"She's in the back by the boys' department. It's always nice to see you, sugarhon. Love your haircut!"

As I start walking toward the back of the store, I say, "Hope you get those glasses."

I can't help myself. Why can't I stop talking? It's like I have some disorder—Always Be Nice and Fill *All* the Silences.

"Already bought, sweets."

And then I see my mom. I hold my breath as I approach. "Hi, Mom."

She turns around to look at me. She smiles. So far, so good. She inspects my head.

"Turn around." She runs her fingers through the back of my hair.

"Mom. Not here," I whisper.

I'm mortified that someone will see. It's bad enough that I have to bring myself in here to show her my haircut for approval. Once or twice, she's taken shears to my head after a professional haircut because it didn't meet with her standards. This is the first year she's allowed me to start getting it cut outside the house. She claimed the reason she cut my hair was to save money, which is probably semitrue, but she also said she didn't want me to have any of that *girl style which would please the devil*.

"It's good. He did a good job. Short. Just in time for Greek school. Don't want you going there with long hair. Shameful," she says as she squints and inspects my face. Then she frowns.

"What?"

Shit.

There's never a clean finish. She can never end with kindness.

"You should sleep with a clothespin on your nose. Especially when you have short hair. It highlights the bulbousness and the large nostrils. You can really notice it now that you're getting older. Everything is growing, including your already too large nose." She turns around and continues to fold sweater vests.

This.

The "turn." Even a hint of a compliment, a crumb of kindness, or a smidge of love has to be balanced with some "truth."

She still has her back to me. "I used to sleep with one when I was your age. Your nose never stops growing. You need to tame it. It's not a good look. If I could afford it, I would get a nose job. Only your family will tell you the truth. The honey-soaked lies you want to hear only come from strangers who can't love you."

Gaige told me he loved my nose. That it gave me character. That it suited my face.

She now turns around to look at me.

"You may have an opportunity to make money one day. If you do, we can both get nose jobs. Now go home and eat. Don't forget about Sunday. Your aunt Lena and uncle Tasos are also coming over. I have been witnessing to both of them, and your aunt is almost there. Tasos, well . . . he's of the world. The Lord is moving through her. It would be a miracle to have one of my sisters find the Lord." Her smile goes away. "Did you let the gay touch you?"

At first I think she's actually read my mind. I freeze.

She doesn't seem to notice. She turns around. She has graduated to sweater folding now. "Did he touch you while he cut your hair?"

And then I breathe out. Of course. *The gay*. Any man who works at a job that my mother deems to be woman's work must be gay.

"Mom, he didn't—"

"You have to be careful. Those men are predators." She continues to fold sweaters.

How does she do that? Go from talking about my hair to something so much more . . . alarming.

"He just did his job."

"You know I worry about you. What's best for you."

I start to feel dizzy. Maybe it's the way she whipped so quickly from subject to subject. I can see her, hear her, but it's like I'm underwater. My right hand starts to feel numb. The numbness moves up my arm.

"Go straight home. No adventures or daydreaming."

I walk home in a daze, avoiding any reflection of myself, and go right into my room.

seven

The three of us are sitting in the dining room. My father is eating as if he hasn't seen food in days. For a man who works around food all day long, he always comes home hungry. My mom is slowly cutting her chicken.

"Tomorrow after work, I need you to help me with my hair." She's looking right at me.

"Mom, I have homework."

"You can do both. I need this curl relaxed. I want it settled by Sunday, when everyone comes over. I can't reach the back myself."

"This kind of stuff takes time." I'm stabbing my potatoes in the sauce. This is one of the many times I wish I had a sibling, someone else who could take some of the focus off me.

"Don't tell me how it works. You are helping me with my hair and that's it. Your father works two jobs. Kills himself for you, and you can't do one simple thing."

I'm looking down at my food and say, barely above a whisper, "Mom, this isn't a two-person job. I have stuff and you can go to the salon for—"

I can feel her eyes on me. She speaks in a clenched-mouth sort of way that makes me believe she's talking about more than her hair. "You're an awful person, even a worse son. You know money is tight. Did your father tell you they cut his hours at the restaurant?"

My dad is still eating. Head down. *Way to get in there, Dad, and try to defuse the crazy.*

With my fork I adjust the food on my plate and say under my breath, "Like that's a new one."

"What did you say to me?"

My father finally speaks. "Voula. Let's just eat." He turns to me. "Nice haircut."

She grabs my left ear. I freeze. Her hand, still grasping my earlobe, moves down the side of the ear and lands on the bottom of the lobe. She squeezes her fingers and yanks down.

I keep my head down.

Don't cry.

Breathe.

She speaks in short, calm, calculated breaths. "Why is he so disrespectful?" She's looking at my dad.

"Voula. Please. Stop."

"You should be outraged. He's not a good person, your son." With that last word she yanks on my ear and releases her grip. That energy slams my head face first into the edge of the table. Somehow I'm able to quickly move my head toward my chest just enough that my nose misses the table surface and my forehead takes all the force. I lift my head back up. Oh, too quick. Literally seeing stars. I blink several times and look over to see her calmly cutting her chicken. I try to focus my eyes toward my dad. He's looking right at me. He's paralyzed. I can tell he's upset, but he doesn't do anything. *Why? Why don't you say something, Dad?* Maybe we're all so used to this that we just fall into place—into our roles.

"Evan? You okay?"

My head is swimming. I can feel something warm dripping down my face.

"I'll get some ice." My dad starts to move his chair back.

"Sit down, Eli." She's still working on her dinner.

"Voula, this is too much."

I pick up my napkin and put it on my forehead. Blood. I leave the table and go into the kitchen for ice and a paper towel. I bend over and look at my reflection in the toaster. I look closer. It's not a lot of blood. It looks like a single cut but definitely the beginning of a bruise. Now pain sneaks in.

"We're not done. Come back in here and sit back down." Her mouth is full and I can hear her put her fork and knife down onto the plate. After any kind of violence my senses are hyperalert. Every little thing is magnified. I can practically hear her breathing from the other room.

As I enter the dining room I hear my dad. "Vee. No more."

"Don't tell me—"

"No!"

"You don't see what I see. Just look at him. Really look."

"I only see our son."

I sit back down at the table. She turns her face toward mine. "I thought this year, this year at Bible camp, would be the time God got through to you. Even He's given up."

Looking down, I muster, "Mom, I don't—"

Her face gets closer to mine. "You came back even more like a gay. The way you walk. Talk. Your clothes. The obsession with your hair."

I close my eyes. Her voice starts to rise as she continues, "It's Satan's world. The gays marry, have children, men are women, women are men. You want this evil for your son? You should be helping me. We need to protect him."

"Voula, it's a different time."

"I asked the pastor to help me. But I have to do everything myself. I work. I clean, cook, and I'm trying to save this. This"—she spits three times in my direction—"this deviant from himself and that lifestyle."

"Vee. Honey." He's almost pleading now. "Please, let's just have a peaceful dinner."

"What? Are you a *pousti* too?" Her voice is harsh and accusatory. The word *pousti* is Greek slang for gay—and not in a kind, understanding sort of way.

"Voula!"

I hear him get up. I grab my paper towel filled with ice, place it on my head, and turn my back to the dining room. I can hear him walking toward the stairs and at the same time I sense her coming up behind me. I lunge to the side and she slams into the sliding glass door in the kitchen that leads out to the patio. The plate she was holding smashes into the door. Plate fragments everywhere. She turns to me, furious.

"You're a *pousti*! An evil *pousti*!" She lunges at me with what's left of the plate. I fall backward with her thrashing above me. She's hitting any part of my body she can while I'm trying to knock the jagged remains of the plate out of her hand.

It grazes my arm and it fucking hurts. "Mom!"

Shit. Now I'm bleeding there, too.

My dad jumps in and tries to wrestle her off. I quickly half crawl, half walk to my room. Breathing heavily, I manage to shut the door. I can still hear her screaming. It's directed at me and at my dad. It sounds like she's trying to get away from him. He must be restraining her. She starts to sob.

A surge of anger rushes through me—at my mom for never changing, my dad for standing by, at myself for allowing it. Then I'm suddenly overwhelmed with guilt—I fought back this time. I feel hot with rage and nerves—am I capable of violence? What if I'm just like her?

eight

There's a knock at my bedroom door.

"Open. Please."

Her voice is meek. I'm on the floor leaning up against the foot of my bed with my notebook in my lap. I'm drawing her standing over me. She's reaching for my head with both hands. Usually when I sketch a scene like this I'm faceless, with no recognizable features—like one of those CPR dummies. But this time, I draw my hair. The way it was before the haircut. My wild, crazy, Greek-fro hair. When I'm drawing in my notebook, it's the only time I'm totally honest.

"Do you want to make cookies with me?"

I scribble the mess of hair on the sketch of myself with more intensity. I take my right thumb and press down on the paper, smudging the charcoal to create shading.

After any incident like this she reaches out with things she knows I like. When I was really young and something like this would happen, she'd make my favorite meal afterward, or we'd go to the local department store and look at all the toys. We couldn't afford to buy anything, but looking at them was enough. She'd buy me a candy bar instead. I would be lulled into believing it would be different next time. That she loved me.

It never took, of course. And nothing ever changed. Now, none of it works anymore. It stopped working a long time ago. I've been oddly numb to it and even to the pain, but tonight I felt it all.

She speaks softly. "I'm going to make kourabiedes. Your favorite. Come into the kitchen and help me. If you want."

Her footsteps fade into the kitchen and I can hear drawers being opened. I look at my phone. Nothing.

"Evan?"

"Not now, Dad."

"How's your head?"

"You tell me."

"What else got hurt?"

"Everything."

nine

3:24 a.m.

I'm wide-awake.

I'm so wired—it's as if there are different Evans, all with completely different plans percolating inside me.

I walk over to my door, hold my breath, and listen. Nothing. I look under the door. Completely dark. I grab my notebook and phone, slowly slip into my laceless Chucks, and make my way to the window. Even though it sucks in the summer to be without window and door screens—mosquitoes are pretty much part of the backdrop around here—it's times like these that I'm grateful for my father's procrastination. I lift the window as quietly as I can and tuck the notebook into my pants and my phone into my pocket. The key is to grab a firm hold of the tree with one hand and use it as leverage while closing the window with the other. For a minute or two it looks more precarious than it actually is. It's just one story.

I've fallen from higher. Plus I already look pretty bruised up, which means if I fell I wouldn't have to lie about my appearance later at school. I swiftly climb down and head to the back of the house. My bike is under the kitchen porch. I grab it and start riding.

I'm riding so fast that my face tingles like crazy.

I can see the monastery. It's less than a few blocks away and I'm pedaling with as much force as I can. It's used as some kind of part-time storage facility for farm equipment. I get off my bike. I'm winded and now everything is tingling, not just my face. I walk with my bike to the right side of the building and head toward the back. There are very tall windows that start about three feet above ground and then go down under the surface at least another three feet. It looks like it's a partial basement. I prop my bike up against the wall, get on my stomach near the cutout by the windows, and, in one swoop, flip into the space below the ground. I'm right outside one of the tall windows. I reach for the window handles and jiggle them. When they give a little, I look behind me, just to check I'm alone. I slowly open the window and slip inside.

I've been coming here for years. This room is filled with statues, like at least fifty of them. The very first time I discovered them, it was sensory overload. Talk about feeling like everything is trying to communicate with you—every statue seemed like it had something to say.

Some of the statues have their hands outstretched, others

are holding goblets or books. Others seem to be in the midst of battle and some are just hanging out. In robes. Mingling. As they do.

Over the years, I've given them roles to play. The statue with the outstretched hands has a very noble face. He looks strong. I always thought of him as the one who would find a way to lead me out. Out of this town. This life. I'm still waiting.

The female statues holding books and goblets are in charge of my future.

The warrior statues, the ones in battle, are many. They are imposing. Formidable. I've decided they can be my army.

I pull out my notebook and sit in the middle of the room. I grab my phone and put it on the ground in front of me, when the screen lights up. There are three texts from Henry:

Ru up 4tennis 2morrow?

Mom wants 2no-can u do dinner our house this wknd?

Down 4 icecrm?

Yes, to all of it, but I can't. Can I?

I open the notebook.

Every day there's at least one entry.

September 8

I close the notebook. I don't know what to write. Things had been feeling like they might actually be going okay for a while. Now it's . . . too much. Everything is too much.

When the beatings were at their worst, I used to think of ways to die. Usually, I hoped that she would just go too far one day and kill me. It would have been easier. That was about two years ago. Since then I've grown. I'm now taller than she is, plus it's getting more difficult for her to explain the bruises. The cuts. The burns. They threaten to disrupt the story of the perfect Greek family. I thought the beatings had been replaced by more insults and psychological mind games. I allowed myself to relax a bit. A dream of a different future was starting to take root. But today proves that all of it was just temporary.

I open the notebook and flip to the next blank page. I start to draw the statues, but not in this room. I draw them out in the world—in the same poses, but free.

I flip through the notebook again and stop on an entry from this summer's Bible camp.

June 19

It's only been a day and already everything is fucked. Gaige was assigned as my study/workshop partner—he's a year older, from California. Way too friendly, big sexy smile and a swagger that was making it difficult for me to concentrate. Maybe I can get a different partner . . . like the kid who smells like hot dogs could work. Liam? Tomorrow I request Liam!

*Apparently his name is Limm. Really, God? Limm?
And changing partners isn't allowed.*

My phone starts to ring. It's my father.

"Where are you? Do you want to go get doughnuts?"

"I went for a bike ride."

"You should come home before your mother wakes up. Do you want me to wait?"

"No. I'm heading back now."

I hang up and look at the next entry.

Gaige and I kissed.

ten

A boy kissed me and I kissed him back.

Gaige had asked me if I wanted to go for a walk. I was slightly hesitant because I had a feeling I knew what could happen, but what could happen was also the reason I wanted to go. Ten p.m. was curfew. Everyone had to be back in their cabins by then. Gaige and I shared a cabin with two other guys, and around midnight, they were asleep. So we snuck out. We didn't walk far—just a few yards—before he clumsily grabbed me and kissed me. It's not like I wasn't thinking about it. Hell, I thought about it the first time I saw him. There was this geeky but confident sexy way he talked and walked. He also knew so much about stuff I never even thought about.

I couldn't believe that after imagining it for so long, I was finally kissing a boy. So I went for it. I kissed him like I needed it to live. So much so that he must have thought I wanted more.

But I didn't, at least not then. One kiss was exciting and dangerous enough.

Coming back home meant that I could escape those feelings. Leave behind what happened at camp. Now, Gaige is here and my best friend has turned hot. What the hell, God?

"Wait up! Panos!"

I stop riding and look behind me. Jeremy.

I say, "I just saw your text this morning. Sorry . . ."

"I figured you were deep into some homework or tennis with Kimball." He's come up beside me. His eyes widen as he sees my face. "What the fuck? You are the clumsiest dork. What did you do to your head this time?"

I give a forced laugh. "Oh, you know."

Jeremy buys it. He always does. He rolls his eyes and says, "Rode by the courts. No sign of you and the Kimball there. Being studious?"

We're walking our bikes toward the school entrance when I spot Henry coming up from the far left. I can tell it's him by his long gait. "Just trying to catch up on all the homework."

Jeremy says, "Jesus, Kimball's in a hurry."

"Hey, guys." Henry is out of breath.

Jeremy nods. "Hey."

But Henry's looking at me. I say, "Sorry about not getting back to you. I just saw the texts this morning."

Jeremy won't shut up. "Panos, as you know, is a real social animal. He ignored mine too. You're not alone. He's too busy studying and falling into shit. Okay, my work here is done and I still want to go riding. This weekend? The trails? Kimball, you're welcome to join." Jeremy looks at me.

So I say, "Yeah. Let's figure something out." Why am I lying?

And just like that, Jeremy is a block away. He moves as fast as my insides feel.

Henry looks concerned. He reaches for my shoulder, I back away. He says, "What happened to your head?"

"Nothing. Just . . ." I dismiss his question with a wave of my hand.

"Maybe you should get it checked?"

"It's just a small cut. Nothing to get excited about." I hate lying to him, but at this point it's second nature.

"I mean the falling. It happens a lot. Maybe you should see someone."

"I don't think there's a doctor for clumsiness. Hey, what was the urge for ice cream last night?" I'm trying to change the subject.

"Tonight? Bugle's? I think it's the last week it'll be open late. Still a week of summer hours. It's tradition."

Bugle's is where everyone in town goes for ice cream. It's the best and not just because it's in our town. The town has next to nothing that's any good, let alone *the best*. When I leave Kala-kee, Bugle's is one of three places I will truly miss. The other two are Jasper's Pizza and the monastery.

"Let me see what time could work . . ."

"Pick you up at the corner."

"I'll text you."

We never meet at my house. Even at my front door. It's an unwritten rule that all my friends know. In all the years that I've known Henry—hell, in all the years I've known anyone—no one has been to my house more than a handful of times and *never* inside. Jeremy came in once. It was summer and the front door was open because it was a record heat year and we don't have AC. He called my name from inside the front door and my mother appeared out of nowhere and scared the shit out of him. He always waits for me across the street now and texts me when he's a block away. She won't forbid me to see my friends due to the optics. It has to *look* like we're normal. But she'll make it as uncomfortable as possible.

"Are you going to the atrium? I'll go with you."

"Okay." Only I don't want Henry to come to the atrium with me.

I lead the way, and once we're inside, Henry says, "Are you avoiding me?"

Yes. But out loud I say, "What? Yeah, right."

I take a seat on one of the benches.

Henry is staring at me in his Henry way. "Ever since you

came back from camp this summer you've been—"

"It's been crazy. Right? Between work and stuff, I haven't had much time."

"What's going on? I've barely seen you since being back. Something happen at camp?"

The thing is, I wanted to tell him. Tell him as a friend before I went to camp. Before he made me feel like this. Before he looked like this. Instead I say, "It was just camp. You know— very Bible-y."

He looks at me oddly but shakes it off. "Being at the Kimball pool this summer was not the same without you."

"I missed the pool." I missed him. "The lake was so disgusting at camp. Also, I missed your mom's lunches." Mrs. Kimball makes great lunches. They aren't anything particularly out of the ordinary, but they are to me because it's not Greek food. A grilled cheese at the Kimballs' by the pool is magic. *And Henry.*

No thinking about Henry.

Especially by the pool.

In swim trunks.

I've seen him in swim trunks hundreds of times—hell, I've already seen him naked when we used to go camping and change in the same tent. It was different then.

I tell myself to focus on the plants inside the atrium.

"Did you know that Virginia bluebells this time of year are rare? Blooming. Rare to bloom."

"What?"

"Just a fact."

What am I saying?

He smiles. "You're so weird. Honestly. And I missed the weird." He runs his left hand through his hair, which doesn't help my increasing distraction. He blinks a few times, then refocuses on me. "Anyone new this year at camp, or just the same church kids?"

"Same." I say it so quickly, it's more like a sound than a word. "You know, the usual suspects." *Oh, and a new boy I kissed instead of you.*

We are never quiet. Henry and I can literally talk about anything. I don't mean anything as in *anything personal and private*, though he has shared more with me than I ever have with him, but any ridiculous subject we can discuss for hours. We once talked for at least an hour about how you can never have enough pockets on shorts. We were close to literally drawing up plans for shorts with more pockets than you could imagine. Hidden pockets. Pockets inside pockets. That's how into it we were.

The silence is making my eye twitch. I break it by blurting out, "How's Amanda?" He looks at me, confused. "I mean, how are you now that you guys are broken up?"

He shrugs his shoulders. "I dunno. It's—she just pretends nothing ever existed between us. I've been completely scrubbed from all aspects of her life."

"What happened?"

"I guess . . . We're different. Too different."

His turn to abruptly change the subject. "Any girls at camp?"

I nervously half laugh. "We should head to class." I look at my phone to check the time. There's a text from my uncle Tasos. Great timing.

Your friend Gaige is in town and will be at church this Sunday. I'll tell your mom and dad to invite him to the house after. He's nice.

I read it three times. I read it again. Henry finally leans in and says, "Is something wrong?"

I jump about a foot.

"I gotta go. See you later." I'm practically running out of the atrium.

"Bugle's. Don't forget!" Henry yells back at me.

I'm barely out the door and into the hall when I hear, "Evan!" It's Tess. If a voice could ever match a hair color, bright blond, it would be Tess's. I turn around but still keep walking. Backward.

"Tess. Hey."

"Evan, stop." Tess seems annoyed.

I keep going. "Gonna be late."

She runs to catch up with me. Until I'm forced to stop just short of a water fountain.

"You get weirder every day. Were you in the atrium?"

"No."

"I just saw you." Tess looks right at me, as if she's searching for truths.

"I meant, yes." I'm fumbling.

"With Henry?"

"Um. Henry?"

"Yeah. Henry went in there with you."

"Right. We were trying to figure out—"

"There you are." Kris walks up to us and says to Tess, "I've been looking all over for you."

Tess smiles at her. "Perfect timing, Kris." Back to me: "I know you and Henry have always been close. Kris and I were wondering if Henry's still with Amanda. All photos of Henry are off of Amanda's social media and—"

Kris gives Tess a look before saying, "*I* don't wonder about Henry."

"I don't know what the deal is," I tell them.

"Well, let's do a little walk and talk on the way to class and maybe your memory will be refreshed." Tess links her left arm into my right and leads the way.

eleven

Entering my house is always a tricky proposition.

I never know when she's going to be home. Also, this is the *day after* an incident. The day after is always up for grabs. I'm halfway up the staircase and so far no noise is coming from upstairs. I exhale, quietly.

"I'm in the living room."

Shit.

"Come here." Her voice sounds like it's coming from the sofa.

I'm at the top of the stairs now and I can see her. She's on the sofa, legs off to her right side and slightly tucked under one of the sofa cushions. All the drapes are closed and she only has one table lamp switched on. There is a dish towel draped over the shade, and what's left of the daylight is streaming in from where the drapes don't meet. She's wearing her dark-blue terry-cloth bathrobe with a light-pink nightgown underneath.

When she's in this outfit midday, it's a sure sign that she's not feeling well. She must not have gone into work today. The belt of the bathrobe is wrapped around her head. She uses it to help alleviate migraines.

"Sit down, please." She motions to the chair next to the sofa. Her voice is calm and collected, which is even more scary. I take a seat.

"How was school?"

"Fine."

"Your uncle Tasos called. He met one of your Christian friends from Bible camp. Greg?"

"Gaige."

"Why didn't you tell us about him? Why not give him your number? He has to track you down at your uncle's?"

"He lives in California."

"He's a good Christian boy. Not Greek, but at least a Christian. Right?"

Ugh. The fuckery. On so many levels.

Being a Christian makes up for so much that even if you happen not to be Greek, you're still in the running to be accepted by the Panos Family.

"The Lord helped him remember that you mentioned your uncle's restaurant. The boy is here for a tour of the Loomis Bible College in Chicago."

"Oh. Good."

Not good.

"You should see him while he's here. Maybe bring him over for dinner while we still have this house. Has he ever had Greek food?"

So completely not good. "I think he has. He likes it."

"Who doesn't like Greek food? You even like it." Under her breath: "You don't like anything."

"I like a lot of things."

"Nothing your father and I do. This is the kind of people you should be hanging out with. Gaige. This kind of influence."

She looks at me for a second with her mouth so straight and flat. Then, the corners turn up slightly. She leans in. *"You can't hide."*

I want to get away but I force myself to try and act casual. "A bunch of kids from school are going out tonight. It's the last week that Bugle's will be open."

It's like she hasn't heard me. "Your father can pretend or genuinely not know . . ." Her voice is calm.

"What?"

"But I know you have evil in you."

The palms of my hands are drenched in sweat. "Mom, I'm trying. I don't . . ."

She leans back and continues to speak calmly and with purpose. "You have to be willing to do the work. It's heavy lifting and it requires constant attention. You can't be lazy."

"No." Anything to get her to agree to my getting out of here.

"I want you to see Gaige. Show him the you that is good." She looks toward the kitchen, lifts her hands, and runs them through her hair. "Who is going out tonight?"

She's still looking away.

"Um, you know. The usual. Jeremy, probably Tess—the girl he likes—and Lonny Cho, Scott, Gabe, their girlfriends . . ."

"Beans too?"

My parents tend to describe people before they even try to remember their names. They find the one defining characteristic and then call them that from that day forward, even after they've learned their real name. To this day, my mom refers to Henry as "Beans" because she thinks he's built like a string bean. (This was prior to his new, more muscular physique, of course). My dad used to call our immigration lawyer "Onions" because he would smell like onions in the summer when he sweated. Jeremy is "Fire Hair." Red hair. Original.

"Yes. Probably Henry's sister too." I'm sure Claire's not coming. She's away at college. As far as I know it's just Henry and me, but it helps to have a solid male-female mix when trying to get permission to do something with secular, non-Christian friends.

"I can help with your hair tomorrow?" I offer with as much warmth in my voice as I can muster. "Friday is enough time to help relax the curl by Sunday."

She's looking down at her robe and picking at the little worn fabric balls that accumulate on any old piece of clothing. "Not too late. Invite Gaige. He left his number with your uncle." *I have his number.*

Okay. I can handle this compromise—I'll text and invite him. Also, I'm doing everything in my power to not express any sign of excitement about her allowing me to go out. After an incident like yesterday's, her behavior tends to go one of two ways.

She feels guilty and will agree to a lot in order to make up for what she did.

Or she is in such a downward spiral that anything, *anything*, will set off a greater and more intense scene.

Thankfully, number one is where we are right now.

She looks down at the sofa cushion and brushes the fabric with her hand. All the fibers need to be lined up in the same direction. "I wept the whole train ride to Greece from Austria on our way to pick you up."

I've heard this story my whole life. My first four years were spent with my father's parents, in Greece. My parents both worked and lived in Austria. They went there because jobs were hard to come by in their own country.

"You were so small. Maybe your grandmother didn't feed you properly, or you wouldn't eat. I don't know. Do you remember?"

I nod. I do remember.

"You were scared to come to us. You held on to your grandmother's apron with one hand and your grandfather's pant leg with the other and just looked at your father and me as if you didn't know who we were." She starts to cry. "Your eyes were big. So wide. I'll never forgive myself for leaving you."

"Mom . . ."

"It's why you're not close to me. You didn't want me. You resented me."

"I don't—"

"You still do. It's my fault. We needed the work. I didn't know what to do with you, and when I finally got you, it was too late. You had already decided to hate me."

I think about how all I wanted was to feel safe. To be loved.

She's so small when she's like this. So vulnerable. So harmless. She looks right at me. "You still have big, beautiful eyes."

twelve

I can sense her looking out the window at me. She's waiting. Waiting to see if Henry pulls up by himself. Even if she can't see all the way to the end of our street, she'll still look as if she can. I head to the corner with my notebook tucked deep into the front of my pants. I feel uncomfortable leaving it in my room now. There's the 1995 Subaru Legacy L wagon (spruce green, pearl metallic exterior, with a gray interior) turning onto our street. Henry inherited the car from his mom. He pulls right up in front of me, reaches over, and unlocks the passenger door. I get in and try to act casual.

"Hey."

"Hey," Henry says as I get in, and then proceeds to drive down our street toward my house.

"What are you doing?"

"I'm making a very long U-turn."

Trying to sound normal I say, "Um, why?"

As he passes our place I can see my mother still looking out the window. She now has it open and is leaning out, her head following the car's every move.

"Is that your mother?"

"Yep. Thanks for the pickup—could have met you there."

"Course." He looks over at me, turns the wheel of the car so abruptly that it makes the Legacy squeal mid U-turn. Once turned around, he floors it and we race out of my street so fast I'm forced back deep into my seat. "There," he says.

"What was that?" I ask, exhaling a bit.

"It gives her something to see." He laughs a little. "Nice haircut." He goes to rub my head, but I pull away. I don't want him to feel any possible lumps or bruises.

"Sorry, just jumpy."

He doesn't push it. "You gonna do the standing Bugle's order tonight? Sundae?"

"Yep." I try to casually reach into the front of my pants and remove the notebook.

"Planning on doing some homework?"

"I was doing homework when I left the house so I just brought my notebook." That could not have been a worse excuse.

Luckily, I don't think he noticed.

"I'm struggling with mine in Mr. Crandell's class."

"P.E.?"

He shoots me a look. "You know he used to be an English teacher."

"Right."

"He wants us to write what's inspiring about being an athlete. He says it makes you a better athlete if you write what you feel. Then it becomes real inside you . . . makes for a . . ."

"Yeah. We got that too."

"Did you write something? I don't know if it helps."

"I wrote about stuff but it's different. I'm not actually going to make sports a career or anything."

"This doesn't inspire me—writing about it isn't gonna make me want it more, is it?"

"You don't sound convinced."

"It's not that I'm not. Convinced, I mean. I just don't know where to start and I've got zero motivation. I don't know. I was hoping you could motivate me with some great idea. Something. You're the creative one. Plus, dude, you don't really have to worry about his homework 'cause he knows you don't give a shit about any kind of sports."

"Fuck you, asshole. I play tennis with you all the time. And that doesn't get me off the hook. I still have to do the homework."

"Dude—you just said you aren't going to make it a career. Damn, chill out. And you haven't in forever."

"Haven't what?"

"Played tennis with me."

"Is this supposed to make me want to help you?"

He looks ahead and doesn't say anything. Only his right hand is on the wheel. His left is resting out the window and he's moving it with and against the wind. I know his arms are long, but they look extra defined tonight. He's wearing a white short-sleeved T-shirt and he's still tan from summer break. His shorts are loose and faded in spots, and he's wearing black Vans slip-ons that have seen better days. The whole thing is making it difficult for me to concentrate on anything other than how sexy he looks to me right now.

Henry breaks the silence. "I'm just frustrated."

"I'm a little tense too. I can help if—"

"You look ready for the winter," he says, glancing over at my bulky sweatshirt, which looks even bulkier thanks to the two T-shirts underneath. I figured out a long time ago I should cover myself as much as possible to avoid any questions.

"Thought it might be getting cooler tonight. It's officially fall, right?"

"There's a few more weeks before it's officially fall. We're still in the last days of summer. You know I'm gonna keep this feeling going for as long as I can."

Henry has been known to wear shorts even when there's snow on the ground. He's not afraid of having people notice him, but it's not like he's trying to be noticed. He just doesn't care if they do. I admire that.

He goes, "I don't mean to be all Jason Bourne, but I think someone is following us. Every turn. Every move and this car is right on my ass."

What. The. Fuck? It's my parents. I know it without even turning around. They've done this before. It's my mom, really, but she doesn't like to drive so she ropes my father into driving and following me. Hopefully, once they see we actually wind up at Bugle's, they will turn around and go back home. I hope the place is packed with people.

"Paranoid much?" I try to laugh but it catches in my throat.

He gives me a look, gives the rearview mirror a look, and then shrugs. "You know Tess Burgeon?"

"Yeah. We're not close or anything, but I think that Jeremy likes her. I mean, I know he does."

"Dude, she's into *you*, not Jeremy."

"What?" I am genuinely shocked. Tess? Since when? She's never anything but condescending tones and glances toward me.

He tries to pull into the parking lot of Bugle's, but cars have totally filled the lot. "I forget sometimes we live in a small town. Everyone's trying to get their last bit of summer."

He maneuvers the Subaru in a three-point turn and speeds out of the lot as if he's not driving a '95 wagon. "Street parking it is. Hang on!"

He goes right past the ice cream shop. I get a glimpse

inside. Everyone is here—Jeremy, Tess, Kris, Tommy and his girlfriend, Bella. I can even spot Patty from the Depot and her husband. Normally, this would freak me the fuck out, but it's exactly what my parents need to see. A crowd. A mixed crowd.

Wait.

A mixed crowd that will soon include a boy from California, invited against my better judgment. But still invited . . . by me.

Do I say anything to Henry or wait for him to find out?

"That's a lot of people. Ev, are you down with just grabbing something quick and going for a drive? I'm not much in the mood to be super social."

When has he seen me being super social? He knows I feel like throwing up every time I have to speak to more than two people I don't know. Also, it's not like he hasn't called me "Ev" before. Hundreds of times. But all of a sudden, it feels different—more intimate. Now when he says it I am pretty much willing to agree to anything. That's a new problem.

"I'm good with that." As long as my parents see us walk in there and join everyone. As long as they don't see us getting back into his car, just the two of us, and driving off somewhere. "But back to Tess. Why would you think she's into me?"

"Because no girl goes around asking about a guy as much as she does about you, without interest. I'm parking here."

We're about two blocks away.

I put my journal under my seat and get out. I look around

and in the distance spot my parents' car driving away. The crowd did its job.

"What kind of questions is she asking?"

"You interested?" He sounds surprised.

"Just curious. This is not a vibe I have *ever* gotten."

"Well, you're not the best with vibes."

"I am excellent with vibes. *Excellent.*"

"Not this kind." He smirks and looks directly at me.

I feel a shiver down my spine. Is he flirting?

"I know exactly what's going on. She's trying to find out if Jeremy's said anything to me about her, and he has. He is all about her."

Henry stops. We're about a block away and he turns and looks right at me.

"Evan, you have no idea what you are talking about. She wanted to know if *you* were dating anyone, if *you* were interested in dating anyone, and if *yoooooouuuu* liked girls." He lingers on that last one and pokes my chest with a very long finger.

"Huh." I laugh uncomfortably. *What does that mean?* I can feel my heart racing.

I shouldn't have worn so many damn shirts. It's like Splash Rapids Water Park under here. I feel drenched. I start walking in the direction of Bugle's, rambling all the way. "Well, this is stupid. Why would she want to know all that? I'm going to ask her myself once we're in there and just get—"

Henry is trying to catch up to me. "Hey, slow down. I don't think she wants you to know that she's been asking. Let's just get ice cream and check out what's going on and go. No one needs to talk to anyone about anything."

I attack the front door. It swings out, and as I pull with all my might, I almost hit Henry with it. I forgot for a minute that he was behind me.

"Dude. Just breathe."

We enter and see what seems like everyone we know in this town. This was not a good idea. Not tonight. Not with everything. *Not with Gaige.*

I steady myself and think, *I can do this*. I have faked it before in tougher situations. I see Jeremy and smile in his direction. I scan the room. No sign of Gaige yet.

"Paaaaaaanos! Thought for sure you'd be a dork studying or something else boring." He turns to Henry. "Hey, Kimball."

Henry nods at Jeremy. "I'm going to get in line. You want the usual, Ev?"

"I'm coming too." I lean in toward Jeremy. "I see your girl is here. Have you guys been talking?"

"I don't know, man. Burgeon is being weird. Kris, too."

"No. You're weird. You need to get in there, get Tess alone, and talk to her, but try something other than obnoxious shit. Be respectful. Seriously."

"Thanks, Pubes. I feel super confident now."

"Just be the good Jeremy. Not the d-bag one. The d-bag is strong within you, but I know you can fight it. Tess should see *that* Jeremy."

"You're being the D right now. Not good at the pep talk, Pubes."

"Be nice to Kris, too. Tess and her are close."

I get in line behind Henry. He is looking intensely at the flavors on the board behind the counter.

"They haven't changed and you know you're going for the usual."

"I'm checking to see what the special is."

"Hey, are you mad?"

Henry turns around. "Ev, don't mess with me. Are you interested in Tess?"

"Shit, not so loud." I'm whispering, scanning the room. Everyone seems to be staring right at us. I smile awkwardly at the people who meet my eyes, and then I turn back to Henry.

"No. I am not," I whisper to him while I try to tamp down the mixture of dread and excitement building up in the bottom of my stomach.

From the back I hear, "Evan!" Seconds later a big bear hug from behind me.

"What would you like?" the girl behind the counter asks Henry.

But he doesn't say anything because he's too busy staring at the arms around my waist.

"Thanks for the invite." With that, the grip releases. I turn around. And now I'm facing him.

"Gaige." He's tall, taller than Henry, and the only person I know with wilder hair than mine. He has the kind of big, perfect smile you see on one of those toothpaste commercials, and his nose is the opposite of mine. Sleek and straight. He's not wearing his glasses.

He says, "Glad we can see each other before I—"

"Are you all together?" Ali, the girl working behind the ice cream counter, is flirty-smiling, but only at Henry. They all flirty-smile at him.

"A hot fudge sundae for my friend. Vanilla ice cream, extra nuts, no cherry. I'll have . . . uh, two scoops of mint chip with lots of whipped cream. No nuts, no cherry, no sauce." Henry's not even looking at me right now.

Suddenly Gaige is introducing himself, and Henry is watching him and also me, and I'm not saying anything, but I reach into my pocket for some cash before Henry stops me with ready, neatly folded bills.

"I got this. I invited you." He then looks at Gaige. "What do you want?" At first I think he means, *What the hell do you want with Evan?* But then I'm like, *Oh, right. Ice cream. He's talking about ice cream.*

"Um, just a chocolate cone, but I've got it." Gaige reaches in his pocket and pulls out a twenty. Henry fake smiles at him and shakes his head. "I got it, man."

Gaige says, "Do you have something going on after this, or you got time to hang for a bit?" He leans in. "I've got beer back at my hotel."

I point to Henry. "We're going . . . we have something that . . . gotta get back home after this. But we can hang later. Before you leave." He shrugs and nods.

Ali smiles sweetly. "You're Henry, right?"

He nods, and smiles back at her. Everyone is smiling but me.

"I'm Ali. We're in physics together." She's still not giving him back his change.

"I know that, Ali. Hi." Even though he's still smiling, he's acting oddly stiff.

Okay. So Henry gets all worked up wanting to know if I'm into Tess or not and now he's flirting with this girl? Really? Maybe it's his way of getting back at me. Either way, it's pathetic.

"I'm having one last pool party this weekend, and if you wanted to come . . ."

"Oh, yeah. That sounds cool." Henry flashes her a big, dimply smile. *Fuck you, Henry.* And *Ali!*

"Oh, and you . . . Kevin? You and your friend are welcome too."

"It's Evan. Thanks. My friend's from out of town." I've

been to Ali's house at least twice. Is she pretending to not re-member me?

"I'm here for a few days," adds Gaige.

Henry says, "That sounds fun. We should all go."

As I stand there thinking, *No, no, we should not.*

"Great. It's going to be on Saturday. I'll get you the details."

All three of us move to the end of the counter to wait for our orders.

Henry looks at Gaige. "So how do you and Evan know each other?" It's like I'm invisible right now. I tell myself, *You have finally mastered the art.*

Is Gaige really going to come to that party?

Are we *all* going? I'm supposed to register for Greek school on Saturday.

Like that—all my worlds are colliding.

As Gaige says, "We met at summer camp this year."

Sorry, Gaige—not that storyline. "He's in town taking a college tour. He knew that I lived in Kalakee. . . . The church his family attends is an affiliate of my family's church—that kind of stuff."

Henry says, "Nice. Evan never talks about his friends from camp."

I think, *Now would be a good time for the rapture.*

"Well, he probably never met anyone like me." Gaige smiles. Big.

"We had stuff in common," I blurt out.

Henry looks at both of us. Is that a hurt expression?

We get interrupted by Tess and Kris, which I welcome at this point.

"Were you guys playing tennis tonight?" Tess is chattier than I've seen her before, like she's anxious or something. *Or like she likes you, Evan.* I smile uncomfortably.

I jump in. "Nope. Work—homework. Are you here with Jeremy?" Of course I know now she's not, but maybe with the power of suggestion I can help make this happen for him if he's too big an idiot to do it for himself. Also, I'm actually happy to move on to this awkward exchange. Anything's better than the one I was just having.

I offer, "We're just here."

"Like a date?" She laughs.

"This should be good," Kris says.

"This is Evan's friend from California. Gaige," Henry says.

"Nice to meet you." Tess inspects Gaige and then Henry, then me.

Kris nods at him. "Hey."

As the girls start chatting with each other, Gaige turns toward me and whispers, "When are we going to get some alone time?"

"Not now," I whisper back, and quickly look around to see if anyone is watching.

Henry turns his attention to Tess. "You and Jeremy are on a date?"

Kris snorts. Loudly.

Tess laughs and twirls her hair. "No, I meant you two. You're here for ice cream after homework, like a date." She giggles again. As if that's funny.

I start to feel my face get warm. Henry turns back again toward the counter. I glance at Gaige and he shoots me an uncomfortable stare.

I stand there saying nothing and feeling all kinds of anxious.

"Here are your orders." Ali is holding Gaige's cone.

"Yep, Tess. Just like that. Is that a problem?" Henry says. She half smirks at him.

"Not a problem at all," Kris assures him, sounding annoyed at Tess.

"All right, then. Hope you can get a date with Jeremy, Tessie," Henry says as he grabs his order. He knows she hates being called *Tessie*. Why is he being like this?

Tess's face immediately turns angry.

"I'm not interested in Jeremy!" she says too loudly. So much so that Jeremy, and pretty much everyone else, hears her. Kris gives her a smirk and walks away.

I glance over at Jeremy and he just shrugs, but I can tell his feelings are hurt.

Tess is still focused on us. Henry hands me my sundae and smiles like a big weirdo at me. Gaige looks totally confused, as if he doesn't know what he's witnessing. Then Henry turns to face Tess, licks the whipped cream that's piled insanely high on top of his mint chip ice cream scoops, and says, "If not Jeremy, who are you interested in, Tessie?" He's just fucking with her now.

"Why would I tell you?" she huffs. "And please don't call me that anymore."

"Why wouldn't you? We're no threat if you think we're dating." He signals with his one ice cream free hand to us. As in *me and him*.

There's a part of me that doesn't like the way he's acting. It's not like him to be so mean-spirited, and what I love about Henry is how kind he always is. But still. Having him say that out loud in front of everyone—even if it isn't true—gives me a thrill.

That immediately turns to panic, though, as I'm trying to control the redness of my face—and at the same time wondering what in the world Gaige must be thinking right now.

All I wanted was a sundae. Just a normal outing. I don't get these opportunities often. Suddenly, I've been pulled into this universe where people are flirting and not flirting and wigging out and talking in circles and just showing up from California. Tess gives Henry an angry face this time before she turns around and heads to the corner where the girls from the volleyball team are cluster-laughing. Kris smiles at me. Like we share a secret.

Henry sticks his spoon in his pocket and keeps licking the whipped cream. He turns to me. "You ready? Nice to meet you, Gaige. See you this weekend."

And I can't help it. I think, *Ready for what?*

I turn toward Gaige. "Um, I'll see you Saturday?"

He nods but looks baffled. "Okay. Maybe. I'm not sure I . . . can we talk before then?"

"I'll text you. I have your number. You gave it to me at camp, remember?"

Gaige looks directly at me and answers, "Yes, I do."

Henry's eyebrows go way up at that. I try to breathe as we walk away.

thirteen

After the awkward exchange in Bugle's, we're now sitting in Henry's car eating our ice cream. With almost every other spoonful he looks up at me. I try not to make noise. I've been known to make these kinds of happy noises when I get lost in the way something tastes, like a constant humming-moaning sound. Henry may have even been the one who pointed that out to me.

"No good?" he asks.

"No, it's great. Why?"

"Can't be that great—you're too quiet. Want to taste mine?"

"Yeah." I take my spoon out, but before I know it he's moving his spoon toward my mouth.

"Here." He feeds it to me and then waits for me to finish it. "Good, right? They are the best here. I'll miss this place." He takes his spoon back and continues to eat. "Why didn't you tell me about Gaige?"

"Well, I didn't think . . . forgot, I guess. I mean, I went to camp with a lot of people, not just him. So . . ." *Okay, rein it in, Evan.* "Are you going somewhere?"

"What?"

"You said you'll miss this place."

"No, just one day. We talked about this . . . one day we'd get out."

I don't like the idea of Henry leaving without me. But that's not why I get quiet. I'm quiet because I'm trying to process what's going on between us right now and what was that spoon thing? Spooning? We're spooning now?

Henry says, "You're not going to offer me any?"

We share food all the time. But we've never shared food *like this*. Do I have to do that spoon move now? What is this move? I feel like it's all too much for me.

He's waiting. So I put my spoon in the sundae and make sure to get a scoop with ice cream, hot fudge, whipped cream, and nuts. It's a skill to get that perfect spoonful.

I lift it and start to bring it up to Henry's mouth. Fuuuuuuck, why did I wear so many damn shirts! I'm sweating so badly again and now my hand is practically shaking.

Henry leans in and takes the spoonful into his mouth. He never breaks eye contact.

"Mmmmmm, that was the perfect ratio."

He reaches under his seat to pull out a plastic grocery bag.

He puts his empty ice cream cup in it. I quickly finish and toss mine in as well.

"He remembered you."

"Who?"

"Gaige. All the way from Cali."

"He's checking out colleges here."

"His family is like yours?"

"Well, they're not Greek." I laugh nervously as I search my brain for something else to talk about. "Why did you keep needling Tess so much back there?"

"Ugh. I don't know. It was a dick move, right? Something about the way she was talking about shit. It really bothered me. I don't know."

He finally starts up the car and begins driving. "Where to, Ev?"

I think about how the monastery would be good right now. I've wanted to tell him about it for a long time but never had the nerve.

"Ev?"

"I'm thinking."

"If you don't come up with a place I'm just going to keep driving till we get to California."

"Would that be so bad?" I laugh nervously, but kind of mean it.

Henry gets silent for a split second, then says, "No. It

wouldn't be bad at all." Then he's quiet for what seems a really long, uncomfortable time.

"Hey! I'm just driving here. Waiting."

"I got it." I take a breath and say, "Have you ever been to the old monastery? It's on your side of town."

"I've been by it. It's abandoned, right?"

"They store large farm equipment in part of it, but there's a whole other section that's just like they probably left it. It's like a museum. There's a room with nothing but statues. Like a party of statues."

"How do you know this?"

I think for a minute and wonder if I should tell the truth. Is it time to tell someone, to tell Henry—everything about me?

"Because I broke in. It was unlocked, but—"

"And you never told me? I live just blocks away and you didn't ever think to say, *Hey, man, how about you come with me to this cool place* . . . By. Your. House! Wow. So many secrets." I can't tell if he's teasing or not.

I can feel my nervous energy. The bottom of my feet tingle and my toes start to go numb. I've thought about telling him all the time. Telling him everything, not just about the monastery but about what happens at home, about what I'm feeling, what I'm feeling about *him*.

"Even after all these years, Ev, I still don't feel like I know you sometimes. And I tell you *everything*. I told you about the stuff with Amanda when that shit show was going on, and yet I'm always left wondering with you. Like Tess. Now Gaige." We're both quiet for a bit before he starts again. "Do you know that in all the time we've been friends I've never been inside your house? Not once. And oh yeah, by the way, my mom has invited you over for dinner tomorrow. I think meat loaf and something."

"You don't tell me everything. You couldn't possibly." His driving has sped up. "Slow down, maybe."

"Tell me something I don't know right now and I'll tell you something."

I try to laugh it off. "See, you don't tell me everything or you wouldn't have anything to share." And then I look around. "Where are we going?"

"The old monastery. I want to see this statue party."

Toes completely numb now. Once we go inside, I'll have one less secret from him. And then, what could happen next? Fuck. I try to wiggle my toes to get the feeling back.

Aside from the light cast from the Subaru, it's pitch-dark out there. We're driving in the middle of farm country and it's quiet and flat for miles.

"Well, I'm waiting." He's clearly not going to let this go.

"So, I'm starting?"

"Stop stalling, Ev."

I'm thinking hard. What can I tell him that isn't so . . .

humiliating? Revealing? When he gets tired of waiting for me to find something to say, he blurts out, "I'm not going to college. At least not for a year." He's looking straight ahead at the road.

"Wait, what? How is this just coming out now? When did you decide this?" I'm genuinely stunned. "What about the scholarship? Do your parents know that—"

Henry jumps in, "Look. My mom and dad both know. They're not thrilled, but they've agreed to it. The scholarship is . . . it's not my thing. Everybody else seems more excited about it than I am. It's starting to feel like tennis is my job now. I love playing. We have so much fun when we play, right? I don't ever want to not love it."

"Sorry." It feels like I should say more but I don't know what.

Henry nods.

We come to a clearing and I see the roof of the monastery pop into view. He pulls into the long, bumpy gravel driveway and it becomes clear that his car needs new shocks.

"Is there anywhere to park up there?"

"I don't think so. I ride my bike here after hours, and there's a gate that's locked. We can climb it, but we can't drive onto the grounds."

"Why have I never seen this side of you? I'm just going to park over here and we can walk the rest of the way."

He pulls off to the far right side of the drive. He parks half on the gravel road and half on a grassy downward slope. I may just fall out when I open my door.

"What side?"

"This living-on-the-edge, breaking-into-an-abandoned-building side. It's probably best if you get out through my door." He climbs out and extends one of his arms to me. *This is ridiculous.*

"I got it, Henry." I grab onto the steering wheel to give myself some leverage, slide out part sideways, and wind up folding into myself. I fall onto the gravel and hit the parts of my body that aren't already badly bruised. The pain is mild compared to the embarrassment I feel right now.

"Are you okay?"

I leap up as fast as I can and start brushing off gravel dust. "Totally fine. Let's get up there. Can't wait for you to see this place." I lead the way.

Henry tries to seem stern as he says, "Do not for a second think that I've forgotten you owe me something I don't know about you!"

"And don't think that we're done talking about you not going to college." I'm running toward the gate. I can hear Henry's shoes on the gravel—he's running behind me. He catches up and we're now side by side. He grins as his longer legs take full stride and he's passed me. Even though he's only about three inches taller than me, in moments like these it might as well be a foot. He leaps and touches the gate before me.

"Ta-da!" He throws his head back and closes his eyes toward the pitch-black sky. His hair, which is usually flopping onto his forehead, is all swept back. I steal a look for a brief second. Here stands the guy who has never judged anything I've said or done, even though I don't tell him anything. Yet there's a part of me that feels he may already know stuff I'm not telling him. And he still doesn't judge.

"Let's climb this sucker." He's starting up the fence. "I'll go first and can help pull you to the top."

"Henry, I've been here hundreds of times and have climbed this fence without incident." I grab onto two wrought-iron bars with both hands. Extra firmly. I don't want a repeat of the car exit. "I don't need help doing something I know how to do."

He's halfway up. "You're telling me that you've never poked yourself with these sharp things on the top?" He's now starting to pull himself over.

"They're called forged spear points, and I have never been poked or hurt in any manner by this fence at all."

"You're such a dork. Of course you know what they're called."

I am at the top and I can feel my phone vibrating in my pocket. I've flipped myself around and my back is now facing Henry. I steady myself on the cross bar just below the spears. Henry is on the ground and I can feel him looking up at me. I may have lied about not being injured on this gate before. But I will *not* be injured by this thing tonight. I hold on tight and let go of the bars, pushing off the cross bar with my feet and landing on the ground below in a crouched ball, right next to Henry.

"Dude, you didn't even look to see if I was there. You could have landed right on me."

"But I didn't. We have to go around back. Follow me."

"I could practically walk here from my house. Why haven't I explored this place? Even more annoying . . . why didn't you tell me about it again?"

"Shh, Kimball. We're done with that story."

I lead us past the front entrance, which looks like a cross between Wayne Manor and a church. We round one side of the building and I guide us with a sharp right in order to go past the hedge wall. Henry's walking beside me like everything is perfectly normal. "It's hard to believe that they store old farm equipment in here. This place looks like it should have something a little cooler going on. How did you discover it?"

My phone vibrates again. I take it out and look down at the screen, trying to move in front of Henry so he doesn't notice. "Told you, one of my bike rides." It's my mother. I turn the phone off and stick it back into my pocket.

"Let's take this path to the building and then we can wind toward the back, where the tall windows are." I motion down a trail that goes past a large fountain to the east side of the monastery.

In the back there are two very large sets of windows on

either side of an even larger set of double doors, in the center of the wall. I point to the last set of windows. As we get closer to that part of the building, we're farther away from the already sparse lighting on the property. Henry takes out his phone and turns on the flashlight function.

"Scared?" he says as he shines the light right into my eyes.

I squint and push his hand away. "Idiot. Point it down at the window."

Henry laughs and points his phone toward the window, and the light shines right inside the room. Once he sees them, he almost jumps back.

"Shit!"

"I told you. There's got to be at least fifty of them."

It almost looks like some of the statues have been moved. I've never seen them this close to the actual window before. The two closest to us are almost touching the glass. Henry jiggles the handle.

"Do the windows open in or out?" He's still jiggling.

"Out. Is it locked?" I grab the handle on the other side. Locked. "Hmmm. Strange. They've never been locked."

"Maybe the party got out of control."

"Where are you going?"

"I'm going to try the other doors."

"Wait for me. It's dark—let me shine the light where you're going. . . ."

I jiggle the handle. Open.

"Any luck?" he says from his side.

"It's open."

"Maybe they're on to you. Maybe we'll have company."

I turn around and grab his phone.

"Hey . . . ."

"I turned mine off. This is easier. I know where I'm going."

This room is not part of the statue room. It's a different room altogether, floor to ceiling, wall to wall of wooden dark-stained, built-in bookcases stuffed with books in every possible direction, a very tall intricate coffered ceiling, and what looks like stone floors. There's a very large old and dusty area rug, and a long wooden carved desk on one side that almost looks like it could have been an altar at one time. There's this gold-leaf finish on it that's very faded and worn off. The high-back desk chair is carved from the same material as the desk, and it has a deep-red velvet back and seat cushions, also faded.

"I feel like I need a library now. I didn't realize that I was missing one," Henry says in his normal, nonwhispering voice.

"You're killing me here." I'm still whispering. "Let's try to lay low."

"No one's here."

"If someone locked those windows, then someone was, or is, here." I move toward the door, "Maybe this leads to the other room."

"Here." Henry grabs his phone away from me. He opens the door and shines the light into what looks like a hallway. "This has to be the door to the statue party. It's the room right next to the library." He jiggles the door handle but it doesn't move. He keeps trying. Nothing.

"Pull on them," I say.

He sticks the phone in his mouth, grabs both handles, one hand on each, and pulls. The doors open. He takes the phone and shines the light into the room.

"Success! Let's go." He closes the doors and we stand there as he shines the light slowly around us. This room is much larger than the office/library one, but it feels smaller. Partly because of all the statues, but also because the ceiling in here is lower. His phone light makes all the dust particles flicker. The walls are all paneled, and on the left wall, from where you enter, there's an all-stone fireplace. The floor is a tiled, ornamental pattern that's very faded in spots. But where it's still intact, it has three borders that go all the way around. All three have some sort of braiding. Each row of braiding is a little different.

"I love this place." Henry looks right at me. "Let's live here."

I'm glad he can't see me blushing furiously in the dark.

He has no idea what he's saying or how it's affecting me. Confusing me. At a time when I don't have the luxury of confronting any of it.

Instead I go into tour guide mode. "Let me show you

around." I motion to him for his phone. Holding on to it, I start to move among the statues. The phone casts a light on them that makes the stone look even more eerie. Depending on the projection and angle of the glow, the faces can look graceful or menacing. The light between the statues makes the air seem as if it's shimmering.

"This one with the outstretched arms is leading the way."

I light up the statue so that Henry can see him, especially the face. The eyes don't look like they are staring blankly. They actually look alive, and if you move slowly, you can imagine them following you. I move toward the front and shine the light on three female statues close together. "These ladies with their books and goblets are holding my future. Now as you can see"—I slowly spin the light all around the room—"there are a lot of guys who seem to be in various positions of battle. These guys I call the Army."

I cast the light toward Henry. He looks around and then looks right at me. He's an arm's length away. "Why the Army? Why not . . . . the Town?"

I hesitate for a minute and then, before I can stop myself, I answer, "They're fighting for my life."

He doesn't look away. Usually, this long a gaze—a direct eye-to-eye gaze with anyone—makes me incredibly nervous. I normally can't hold it for more than a second or two. In this moment, this heart-stopping, palm-sweating moment, I force myself to keep my gaze steady.

"I think this qualifies as the something I don't know about you." Continuing his eye lock. "What do you do here?"

"Sometimes nothing. Other times I draw. Sometimes pretend that everything is normal. Just a single normal day when nothing goes wrong."

I wonder if his eyelashes get stuck together when he blinks. There are so many of them. Upper and lower. He's not blinking. He sits down right there in the middle of the room. I follow his lead and sit opposite him. He crosses his legs, leans in, and rests his elbows on his knees. I'm in a similar position, except my hands are behind me, palms to the ground. I'm leaning back.

"Why aren't *you* fighting for your life?" Now he's whispering.

I don't say anything. I look around the room for a minute, then back at Henry. He reaches into his back pocket. He takes out a crumpled piece of paper and hands it to me.

"Here. I feel like I owe you something else."

I take it from him and unfold it.

"Our list of places we promised we'd go to."

I look at it and then back at him. The flashlight function on his phone is casting shadows on his face in a way that, with his high cheekbones, makes him look like he belongs with the statue party. My hands start to shake, just a bit. Not noticeably but enough to make the paper move. I grip it tighter.

"I remember." I try to steady my voice. "I remember when we started this list."

"I carry it with me almost all the time. Ev, remember when we first wrote these down?"

"We were kids. What, seven?"

"Eight. We hadn't known each other that well at the time, but you spent the weekend at our house. You slept on the floor in my bedroom in a sleeping bag."

"Uh-huh."

"It took a lot of convincing. Your mom was not thrilled."

"It helped that she was witnessing to your parents. She thought she'd convert them. I think I may have been used as a Trojan horse."

"It was the very first weekend without Dillon. That dog meant more to me than anything. I've never cried like that since. I was so embarrassed—and in front of . . ." He stops talking and stares at the floor. He runs his fingers over the tree patterns. "You got up and climbed into bed with me and held me till I fell asleep."

He looks at me. I don't say anything.

"Ev, you did that all weekend every time I couldn't stop crying—when I saw his bowl, or his leash. You said that what we needed was to go someplace new. A new start, even if it was for a day."

He starts to laugh a little.

"Like the underwater petting zoo and submerged airplane in Mermet Springs." We both laugh. "What the fuck was that?"

"I don't know." I'm looking right at him and feel closer to a human being than I ever have before.

"This list, even if we never went to anywhere, made me feel better. You made me feel better."

It's my turn to look at the floor.

"Ev, how do you get your bruises?"

Shit.

I try to remember to breathe. I'm grateful it's mostly dark in here.

He scoots closer to me. "You have never tripped or fallen once when we play tennis, or when you ride your bike."

"I'm prone . . ."

"It always happens when you're at home."

I'm staring at the statues and I shift my body slightly away from Henry. He takes the waistband of my sweatshirt in his hand and pulls me in a bit. I put my head down, still turning away. He nudges himself even closer and starts to slowly lift the shirt over my head. I feel paralyzed, scared, thrilled. I stop him.

"Henry. Please."

How is it possible to be cold and be sweating at the same time? He's close enough that I can smell the mint chip ice cream on his breath. Henry whispers, "Ev, I want to be the one who helps you feel better."

Using whatever willpower I can grab onto, I pull away and say, "No. This isn't what you want. What I want." The truth is, it's exactly what I want but I'm so scared of wanting it and even more scared of actually having it.

Henry immediately lets go of my sweatshirt. And the moment is over.

fourteen

My eyes are closed.

"Merciful Lord, protect this child. Protect his loins. Keep them, him from sin. Keep his mind and body pure." She begins to speak in tongues. Only those truly filled with the Holy Spirit can be touched by this mystical language that only God understands. "Maaaalaaaaneeee kwaaannnntaaaaa moriiiinaaa."

I peek my eyes open and see my mother is sitting on the edge of my bed. Her eyes are closed. Her head is swaying slightly and her tone is hushed. I pretend to be asleep. She continues.

"God of goodness and vengeance, we know You are not just love but also anger. Anger toward the unclean, the lustful, the disobedient. Make this child Yours and guide him with Your holy thoughts, not those of the world."

"Vee."

Now my father's in the room.

"What are you doing?"

"Shhh."

I'm holding my breath and trying to relax my eyelids so it doesn't look like I'm fake-sleeping.

"Vee, get out here."

"We praise you, Holy Father. We trust in Your word that never fails. We live on Your promise to cleanse us and deliver us from evil. This child needs delivering. In Your holy name. Amen."

With that I feel her get up from my bed and walk out, closing the door behind her. They are noisily whispering right outside my door.

"What if he woke up? It would—"

"He needs constant prayer. He got home late last night."

"This is getting out of hand and—"

"Shh! You don't know. I can't trust the pastor for everything. You never know, Eli. You never know. Why don't you look at his notebook? You can read better than I can. Maybe there's something in there that tells us what he's up to."

With that I sit up in bed.

Wait.

Where is it?

"Vee, I'm not going to read his private things—it's not right."

"He's changing. He no longer follows my orders. He doesn't listen."

My heart is pounding. It feels like my blood is pounding.

And then it comes to me.

Fuck!

The notebook. It's still in Henry's car.

"Vee, he's never going to trust us or anyone if we continue like this."

"It's time for you to be up anyway. Take him for doughnuts. He talks to you. Find out what he's up to. What he does when he's not here or at school. I'm tired."

I can hear her go into their bedroom and my dad into the bathroom.

My thoughts are jumping from one thing to another.

If I had let him, would Henry have kissed me last night? Did Henry find my notebook? Worse: *Did he read it?* What do I say to Henry when I see him today? I tell myself I did the right thing last night. But it doesn't feel like it.

fifteen

As my dad and I walk into the Dunkin', I'm trying to focus on him, but it's nearly impossible. I keep seeing Henry's face, so close to mine. Remembering the smell of the mint chip ice cream on his breath. The way he was looking at me, which I keep replaying in my mind. Why did I stop him? He must hate me.

Linda is near the end of the counter pouring coffee for a woman in a gray business suit and a perfect black bob. Linda looks up and glances our way. My gift of seeing everything, hearing everything, is especially heightened today. The whole place and everyone in it is so clear and it all sounds too loud.

"If it isn't my two handsomes. Elias, Evan, how are you boys?"

"We're good, honey." We take our seats near the door. It's weird to hear my dad, even my mom, speak English. It's even weirder to hear my dad refer to Linda as "honey."

"You boys going to get your usual?" Linda asks.

My dad looks at me and I nod.

"Wait," I say. "I'll have coffee this time."

"How was last night?"

"Good." God, this is awkward as hell. "Dad?"

"What?"

"Did you follow me?"

Looking at his hands, he takes a shallow breath. "Yep."

"Why?"

"Just want to make sure you're . . ." He stops himself. "I don't know."

"Dad . . ."

"We won't do it again. I promise." Then, changing the subject and his tone of voice: "Your uncle says that you made a new friend at camp. A Christian friend."

"Gaige. He's in town to check out Bible college."

"Here you go, boys. The usual." Linda places the coffees and doughnuts in front of us. "Enjoy and let me know if you want anything else." She winks and walks away.

"Can I go to Henry's house for dinner tonight? After I do Mom's hair thing."

"No homework?"

"I can do it this weekend."

"Don't forget Sunday. It's all-day-church day. Everyone's coming over to the house after."

I don't ask about the pool party. One thing at a time.

He looks uncomfortable. "We have to talk about Greek school. Registration is on Saturday. And we have to talk about the house."

I start on my doughnut and take a gulp, two, of my coffee. "What about the house?"

"You may be getting too old for Greek school and . . ." He stops himself and takes a swig of coffee. He doesn't look at me as he says this. "We may have to sell the house."

"Oh." The thing about me getting too old for Greek school is a lie. We probably can't afford any of this anymore. The house. My extra schooling. But admitting to that is too demoralizing for my dad. I can't say I'm disappointed about the school thing, but the house? "Are we moving?" Wait, would we be moving away from Henry? My school? Plus my room—the only place in the whole house I feel safe.

He shakes his head while downing his coffee.

"I can work on the weekends at the deli. Maybe that could—"

"We'll talk it over with your mother about working weekends. A real estate agent from the church is coming by later today. I'll be home at three. I'm no longer working the second job at the restaurant . . . they let me go. Not busy enough, they said. I'm just at the bakery now." He takes another sip of his coffee. The thing about my dad, even when bad things happen, he never reacts. But I can see the seething. The discomfort. He wears it all over his body. "The agent understands both Greek and English, so you won't have to deal with the paperwork."

"You know I'm not a real estate lawyer, right?" I'm being a smart-ass, but really.

He takes his first bite of his cruller and says, with a full mouth, "You know the language. I don't understand why you can't explain this stuff to us and fill out the papers. I can only understand so much and your mother . . . your mother is right about some things. You can be lazy."

Don't be this person right now, Dad. I need you to be more than this.

"I'm not lazy."

"Don't talk back to me." He lowers his voice to an angry whisper and looks around to make sure that no one is watching or listening. "I lost my job. We'll probably lose the house, and all you care about is yourself."

I fall silent, and guilt instantly takes over for not recognizing how this must make him feel. I want him to save me, but he can barely save himself.

His voice gets soft again with a little bitterness. "Don't worry. You don't have to translate the real estate documents. The agent will do it." We both stare straight ahead in silence for a few minutes. "Sorry about following you last night." He sounds like he genuinely means it.

I nod.

"She worries."

"Do you?"

"No. What time is dinner at Henry's? I can drive you if he brings you back."

"I'll check with him."

"More coffee?" Linda always shows up at the exact time you need her.

"For both of us." My dad signals to our almost empty mugs. "Is Henry still dating—"

"No, but this girl from Bugle's last night invited him to a pool party on Saturday. He's going to go."

"You?"

"Gaige was at Bugle's too. Mom asked me to invite him. She thinks he's a good influence."

My dad's voice is low. "It's okay to have a—you know. To have someone you like. You should go to the pool party. If Gaige is going, your mom won't mind. He comes from a good Christian family."

"He does. He's a good guy and we don't really know each other very well. Plus I'm not . . ."

"Maybe if he moves here because of college you could get to know each other."

I'm trying so hard not to go full-on red-faced right now. Is he actually cool with this? The mixed messages are coming a little too fast and furious. We finish our coffees and doughnuts in silence and get in the car.

"It'll be good to have a group."

"Dad?"

"If Gaige is someone you can talk to. And you have Henry and Jeremy. It's good."

I don't know where's he's going with this, but I agree. "Yep."

"The people at the church are that for your mother. You know?"

"What about you?"

He shakes his head. "I don't know. Never really felt that way for me. Do you want me to take you home first, or straight to school?"

I want to say something. Something that will somehow comfort my father, but all I can say is, "School. I can do some work in the library."

He pulls out of the Dunkin' parking lot and starts to drive away. Fast.

"Are you mad?" he asks.

"I'm . . . frustrated. Yes, mad. I mean, c'mon, Dad. You think I'm lazy? You agree with Mom and out of nowhere you tell me we have to sell the house. You're apologizing for following me, but . . ." I stop talking and look at him. His face is the usual blank stare when confronted with an uncomfortable moment, but his eyes are anything but empty. "You're right about one thing. I'm making this about me. You must also be so mad—worried."

"I can't give you a good reason why we follow you. I do what I think is right every day. Every day. I work hard. I try to pay all the bills. Send you to school and try to make it all work, and no matter how much . . . how hard . . . everything still feels like it's out of reach. We're on the outside. You're even more on the outside."

Any anger I had dissolves into sadness. Sadness for him and for how difficult it must be to balance so much while trying so hard to make it all work. We drive quietly for the next few blocks. It seems like miles.

"Uncle Tasos said Gaige was a very polite, handsome young man. Does he play sports?"

This is how we move on. We just do. No transitions. "No. He's more of a book/tech guy. I think he wants to study something with science."

"You like him?"

Oh. My. God. So much awkward.

"He's nice. We get along and . . . he's nice."

"Henry and everyone else meet him?"

"Bugle's was packed. He met a lot of people."

"Mm-hm."

I feel hot and cold all at once. I employ the signature Panos family deflection technique. "Are you going to look for another job? You know, if I wind up working weekends—"

"I am. Your work money should be for college. You're going to need it. I don't know how much we can help."

"I didn't expect any help."

More silence.

I reach into my pocket for my phone.

"Have a good day. I'll tell your mother about dinner tonight and the pool thing on Saturday. Come right home after school so you can help with her hair."

"I will. Thanks."

As soon as I walk into school, I race to the atrium. The door is propped open with a large, round, plastic trash can. I need to make my cloudy head feel less foggy. This is the best part of coming to school early—no one is in here.

I find the farthest bench from the door and text Henry:

Hey, I think I left my notebook in ur car. Under my seat. Can u bring it? In atrium.

Please. Please don't read it. Please, Henry. Please.

Part of me also wants to text: *Hey, so . . . how are you feeling about last night? Because over here, I can't stop thinking about it. About you.*

Today feels like one of those days when it's hard being here at school. The kind of day when faking it is harder than usual. I can do a pretty decent job pretending to be normal. I think if you were to ask kids here what they thought of me, they would fall into one of two groups. One group would wonder if they even knew who I was. Like literally have to wonder if I was even a real live kid who went to their school or just some guy who the person asking the question made up as part of a social experiment. The other group would say that I was a shy, awkward kid who keeps to himself.

I take a breath and write out another text.

Hey, Gaige, it's Evan. I should have info on pool party later today. Will send. Hope ur enjoying Chicago. Sorry about last night.

I sit back.

Let me worst-case-scenario this:

Henry reads the journal.

Finds out about my kiss with Gaige.

Discovers the abuse.

Finds out the extent of crazy religion stuff.

Decides it's too much.

Exposes me (is that possible?).

No more Henry.

Worlds colliding.

My phone buzzes.

Gaige.

Cool. Let me know when u do. Want to talk.

I lie down on the bench and think about Henry.

About the monastery.

Breathe, Evan. Think back to the monastery.

Back to Henry.

Back to what almost happened. What did happen.

If we kissed, would it be different than with Gaige?

I hate to think this, but . . . Gaige was almost a test. Why didn't I see this before? *Because you hadn't kissed Henry yet!* A test for me to see. *Do I? Am I?*

My phone buzzes.

I have ur notebook. B there soon. ☺

Oh God. An emoji. He never sends those. Never. What do I say when I see him?

Hey there, buddy, did you happen to read my journal? Then what? What's he going to say if he did? What's he going to say about everything? I wonder if he's thinking as much about last night as I am. Maybe I scared him away from ever attempting to kiss me again. I am freaking out.

"Ev!"

Henry walks in with his big, dimpled smile. Not today. Not now. *Stop it, Henry.*

I smile at him. "Hey." He stands in front of me, slightly out of breath. "Did you run here?"

"Yep. I was clear on the other side of campus. Here." He holds my notebook out in front of him. We're standing so close that his long reach almost hits me in the chest.

I grab the notebook and shove it into my backpack. "Thanks. I was so tired last night I didn't even think . . ."

"So . . ."

Before he can say anything else, I blurt out, "I can come to dinner tonight." I scan his face for any kind of recognition. Any kind of tell that he may know more now in this moment than he did last night.

"Cool. I'll let my mom know."

Nothing.

I think. I can't tell. All my signals are crossed. He couldn't have read it. He's not that good a liar.

"Do you want me to pick you up?"

"My dad's going to drop me off. Can you take me home after?"

"Sure. And we should, maybe, talk about what happened. . . ."

There it is.

"Totally. Oh yeah. *So* important." I don't mean to, but it comes out incredibly insincere. "I agree. We should. Talk."

He looks dejected. Did I do that? "I gotta get to class. Later." With that, Henry exits, and I feel like one of those Illinois State Fair balloons that no matter how full and bright it is while you're at the fair, when you get it home it's completely wilted.

sixteen

"Does this look like anything?"

"Is it supposed to?" I lean into Jeremy's easel and squint at the canvas.

"I don't know, Panos."

"Jeremy, just do what you feel. It's not really about looking like anything."

"Ugh. I feel like you should do this for me."

"Jeremy. Evan. How's it going?" Mr. Quinones, our art teacher, may or may not be on to the fact that I do a lot of (most of) Jeremy's art projects.

"Trying to figure out the best way to do a collage, Mr. Q." Jeremy isn't helping matters. He sounds guilty. Mr. Quinones walks over to our table.

"It's taking shape. This isn't a test, Jeremy. Collages are one of the most free-form ways to express yourself. Don't feel limited. You can mix materials." He looks over at mine, which may be a bit too collage-y. "Mr. Panos here isn't afraid of mixing anything. He's decisive and deliberate with his choice of materials." He walks through the rest of the class and back to his desk. "Let's finish these up before class ends and leave them here. No working on this project at home this weekend."

"Maybe Mr. Panos should be decisive and deliberate with other things as well." Tommy is looking in my direction with his left hand up to his mouth, gesturing oral sex.

"Mr. Goliski." Mr. Quinones sternly motions for Tommy to come up to his desk. "You've earned yourself some new after-school activities."

Tommy rolls his eyes and makes his way up to the front of the class.

"I think he knows, Panos," Jeremy says.

Beads of sweat are forming on my upper lip. I whisper, "Oh my God."

"I think he knows you do my work."

"What?"

"Panos, I told you to scale back. You make my shit look too good. Follow the golden rule: Always, always aim for C+ work when doing my stuff."

"Keep your voice down."

"You going to the pool party tomorrow or do you have Geek school?"

This time I'm the one who rolls my eyes. "Apparently I'm done with Greek school."

"Shit! Since when?"

"Mr. Ludecker? Everything okay?"

"Sorry, Mr. Q. Panos just helped me get a collage break-through over here. Exciting stuff."

"Let's keep the conversations low. People are trying to focus."

I look over at Tommy, who gives me the finger.

Jeremy leans in and lowers his voice. "This is epic. It's a whole new era." For as long as Jeremy and I have been friends, I've been going to Greek school on Saturdays. Between that and helping my mom clean the house, it was nearly impossible for us to hang out on the weekends.

"I think I'm going to pick up extra shifts at the deli. I need to save for college and a car."

"Still. No extra homework. We can squeeze in a ride and stuff. How'd this happen?"

"My dad's down to one job and . . ."

"Classic cutting back. Seen it before. My parents threatened to make my sister and me share a phone last year when they were both worried about layoffs at their jobs. Can you imagine that shit? Sharing a phone? They fucked my world with that. This time that shit has an upside."

Seriously? Jeremy is a classic narcissist and I'm too ex-hausted to deal with him right now. I just say, "Looks like I'm going to Ali's party."

"I guess I'll go too. While the weather's still good. Is that guy from camp coming?"

"Yep. Tess will be there, right?"

"Who cares? You heard her at Bugle's. Everyone did." He lowers his voice even more. "Fucking waste of time."

"Maybe you should have gone with less smart-ass and more—"

"I should have options. I'm in my prime." He leans back on his chair and takes a good long look at his art project, then at mine. "You get this. I don't know how. You do."

Mr. Quinones announces, "Okay, let's start cleaning up. And don't forget the goal for this weekend. Bring one thing from your life away from school to add to this collage." Mr. Quinones looks over at Jeremy and me and motions for me to come over to his desk as he's handing Tommy a piece of paper and sending him on his way. Probably to the principal's office. Tommy shoots me a dirty look.

Jeremy goes, "Never admit anything."

"Thanks. A lot." As everyone files out, I finish packing up the last of my supplies and walk up to Mr. Quinones's desk. "Hey."

"Evan, there's something that I think you should take part in."

"Okay."

"An internship program at a gallery that I'm on the board

of in Chicago. We take three interns every year. It can lead to actual paid work sometimes, but mostly it's just good exposure to art and opportunities. Plus it looks really good to colleges. You're applying to the Art Institute, right?"

I stand there, not really believing we're having this conversation.

"Are you interested?"

"Um. Yes?"

He laughs a little. "It's a good thing. They would want to see samples of your work and you'd have to fill out some paperwork."

"What do I . . ."

"Can you get me a few of your sketches, stuff I haven't seen in class, by Monday? Work you already have. No need to do anything new."

"It's not finished. I mean, I've got a few things, but . . . everything is just . . ."

"That's okay. Gather what you can. We're used to seeing artists' work in various stages of completion. It's less about things being finished. More about process and technique." He called me an *artist*. I don't even call myself that.

I'm trying to think of what I have. What I wouldn't be afraid to show someone else, much less an entire group of people.

"Let me see what I can pull together." And then I pause. "Thank you."

"You're talented. This can be something for you. Not just

the internship, but in life. Art can be something you do in the world."

Now I think he's making a joke. A cruel joke.

"Thanks."

"I'm excited for you."

I go back to my desk, grab my backpack, and head out of class. For a minute I'm not sure I know where I'm supposed to be next. My brain is blank.

"So, did he bust you?"

I jump back about three feet. "Jesus, Jeremy. Were you waiting the whole time?"

"What's up? You can tell me all about it at lunch. Should I give up on my dreams to be a great artist?"

Lunch. Right. "He wants me to apply for an art internship at a gallery in the city. He didn't even mention you."

Henry walks up and falls in next to us. I scan his face to check for signs of—I don't even know. I want to know what he's thinking after last night.

"Panos here is doing some fancy art shit. At a gallery. In Chicago. Mr Q is all over it. He's gay, right?"

"Because he's an art teacher?" Henry fires back.

"Well, yeah, and because he's not married and he's, like, thirty. What?"

"I don't think he's thirty-anything. I think he's still in his twenties," I offer, as if it will prove something.

"What I'm saying here is that all the pieces fit. He's old and not married, or doesn't have a girlfriend as far as we know. He's an art teacher. He dresses nice and his hair is never, ever not camera ready."

"You're an idiot, you know that?" Suddenly I don't want to be around Jeremy. I don't want to hear any more about Mr. Q. "I'm hungry and it's tacos, so . . ." I speed ahead of them into the lunchroom, get my tray, and food and drink, as fast as I can. So fast that I lose them in the crowd. I find a place to sit far, far away in one corner.

I tell myself to calm down. *Jeremy's an idiot. It's like being mad at a baby. Let it go.* Henry finds me anyway.

"How hungry are you?" Henry scoots in across the table from me. "Slight change for tonight. My parents have date night. I forgot. They forgot. Actually, date weekend. It was planned months ago. They're taking in a show in the city and spending the weekend there."

"Oh. No dinner?"

"Yes dinner. We're still on for meat loaf. Mom's making all the stuff and they'll probably still be at the house when you arrive. It's just that it will be you and me. Claire's still at school."

"Okay." I'm not sure how to feel about this. I really wish Claire was going to be there. I like her. Plus she'd be a good buffer.

"Tacos look gross. Panos, I don't know how you can scarf them down." Jeremy slams his tray down on the table.

I shrug, not quite ready to let him off the hook yet.

"So, Kimball, Ali seems to have a thing for you. I could feel her flirting all the way across the room at Bugle's."

Henry says around a mouthful of beans, "You think? Ev, you were right next to the action. In the epicenter, in fact. Thoughts?"

Shoving as much taco in my mouth as possible, I go, "Hmmmmm." And nod.

"The Greek chipmunk over here agrees. This pool party is going to be very good for you, Kimball. A new hookup. A new regular for a new school year. You can be over Amanda for real."

"I am."

"What?" Jeremy isn't the quickest sometimes.

"Over Amanda."

"Even more reason this is going to be good. Panos and I will be going solo." I smile awkwardly and I shouldn't, because my mouth is stuffed with taco meat. Jeremy rolls his eyes at me. "And this is one of the reasons why he's single. Oh, but hey, I guess Panos will have someone there. I forgot about his new BFF, Cage."

I swallow hard. "Gaige."

"That's what I said."

"So he's coming?" Henry asks casually.

"Who?"

"Gaige."

"I think."

Henry's voice is a little higher than usual. "Cool."

My phone vibrates in my pocket. *That's probably Gaige right now.*

"I'll see you guys later." I pick up my tray with one hand and reach into my pocket with the other and grab my phone. I wait till I've walked away from them to check.

It's my mother.

seventeen

There's a car I don't recognize in our driveway. I enter our house with a slight feeling of dread.

"Evan, you're home just in time. Come up, honey, and say hello to Tina." She's always so charming when we're pretending to be the picture-perfect Greek family.

I walk up the stairs as slowly as possible, one. Step. At. A. Time. She meets me at the top of the stairs half mouthing, half whispering, "I tried calling you. The Realtor is here. Behave." She gives me a look. My dad is seated on the sofa in the living room, trays of food spread out on the coffee table. Tina, the woman who must be the Realtor, is sitting, facing my parents, in the wingback chair. I drop my backpack and smile because I can be picture-perfect too.

"Come here, hon." My mother takes a seat next to my father and pats the space next to her on the sofa.

Tina turns to look at me. She smiles. She's very blond. The

kind of blond a lot of the dark-haired women in my family wind up becoming. It's almost white in some parts and then reddish yellow in others. Her eye makeup is heavy with lots of eyelashes and frosted lips. I know this is not a look my mother approves of, but she's shaking her tambourine and making it all seem so "lovely." I smile at my dad and take a seat next to my mom. Too late, I notice my backpack. Across the room. The backpack I should have put away in my room.

"Evan, honey. Don't forget to put away your things." When Tina turns to stare at my backpack lying on the floor, my mother takes her right hand and digs her nails into my left arm. Squeezing harder and harder. I sit there. Quietly. I know the drill. *Don't flinch. Don't move. Don't say a word.* Tina turns around and my mother's hand relaxes on my arm. It looks like she's patting it.

"Voula, you should see my house. I'd be embarrassed. I can never keep up with my boys." She laughs. "I've just given up. What can you do, am I right?" She shakes her head. The way she does it, you can tell she loves her boys in spite of how messy they are.

"Tina, you're so right. It's just a house." The fakeness in her voice is so obvious to me, even if no one else can hear it.

Tina says to me, "Your family has a lovely home. Your room is beautiful. Your mom says you did all that yourself."

"He's artistic, our son." My mother laughs and looks at me *lovingly.*

"Well, we were just wrapping up here. Voula, Eli, any other questions?"

"We'll talk about it and get back to you in about a week or so. Voula? Evan?" My dad looks over at my mother and then at me. I have questions that I don't ask because my questions don't belong here.

"I thank the Lord that you are here to help us, Tina." My mother stands up and goes to hug her. "Please, you must take the rest of the spanakopita and pastries." She leaves to go into the kitchen.

"Oh, Voula, I can't! They're delicious, but Evan just got home from school. He's probably starving."

"Don't be silly. I made these for your family. You must take these to your husband and beautiful boys. Evan has food." She enters the living room holding a few plastic to-go containers and a shopping bag. "Here, I will pack up for you. Your nails are too pretty for you to mess with kitchen chores."

"Your mother is an amazing cook and baker. How are you not fat?" Tina waves her hand at me. Her hand smells of roses. Not real ones, but the drugstore-perfume kind. It's nice. She waves her hand at the top of my head, near the Band-Aid on my forehead. She reaches out, as if she's going to touch it, and I pull away. "What happened?"

"Tennis. He plays tennis. And rides his bike." My mother hands Tina the bag of neatly packaged foods. "He's a clumsy boy. But he's fine." She comes over to where I'm standing and pulls the right sleeve of my shirt down over my arm, to match the left one. Long sleeves. Always long sleeves. "Eli, help Tina to her car." My dad dutifully obliges.

"Thank you again, Voula. Nice to finally meet you, Evan."

"You too." I pick up my backpack and head to my room.

"Evan!" My mother loud whispers once they are out the door.

"Coming."

I find her in the kitchen cleaning up. "You know not to leave your stuff all over. What did you think of her? Help me tidy up before you do my hair."

"She seems nice."

"She's a whore. Did you see how much makeup she wears? Her cheap hair? Hand me that tall glass. It has her lipstick all over it. I have to scrub it to get it off."

"She goes to our church? I've never—"

"Pastor told your father and me about her. Her family attends the later service on Sunday. Too lazy to be up for the Lord in the morning. At least she's Greek. Half Greek, but she understands the language."

My dad enters and starts up the stairs.

"We're in here, Eli. What did she say to you?"

"She thinks it won't be a problem." He reaches into the oven for a leftover piece of spanakopita and my mom swipes his hand away. "But I'm hungry. You gave all the food away."

"This is for dinner. I'll make a salad with it."

"Okay." He turns to me. "What time do you want me to take you to Henry's?"

"We can leave here around five thirty."

"You still going? You're going to leave again?"

"Mom, it's just dinner with the family," I lie. "Nothing big. I can do your—"

"They're not Christian people."

"They go to church."

"Not the right kind. You know that. I've tried for years to witness to them. The mother and daughter wear pants and they let that boy have long hair. Like a *pousti*! You like being around *poustis*?"

"Voula!"

"The Gaige boy sounds like he comes from a more proper family. Why don't you spend time with him? In the right way." She shoots me a look. "You avoid the good and always seek the evil." She spits in my direction three times. "I wish you were never born."

This one is a classic. I've heard it so often that it's like saying *good morning*. It doesn't have the impact it used to. *I wish I wasn't born either. At least not to this.*

"Voula! Enough. What did I say?"

"What? I have no right to be upset? We're selling the house and . . ." She begins to cry. "I'm going to take a very quick shower. I'll call you when I'm ready for you to help me with my hair." She leaves the room, wiping her eyes.

"You know what, she's just—upset. Selling the house is a big deal."

"It's okay, Dad."

"The thing is . . . it's not."

My eyes get wide. "What?"

"She has to stop. I told her. It's got to stop."

"You told her?" I can feel myself holding my breath.

"No more. Right? No more. You have to tell me if she . . ."

"What did she say?"

"Do you like Gaige?" His eyes are getting smaller.

"Dad?"

"You need to be careful. What you say and write."

"Oh." What does he know?

"She wants me to read your journals. I'm not going to do that. I want you to know."

I'm shocked that he's talking like this. Or that he's talking at all.

He continues, "I promised a long time ago to protect her. To make sure she doesn't suffer anymore. I should have made the same promise to you."

"Dad."

"Evan." He gets closer to me and whispers, "I'm having some trouble managing. It shouldn't be like this. You shouldn't have to . . ." He moves back. "I'll be in the backyard when you're ready to go."

Breathe.

From the bathroom: "You ready?"

"Be there in a few."

I grab the curlers from the hall closet and head to the bathroom. She's seated in the tub with her back to me. She's facing the tile. I stare at the back of her head as she removes her shower cap. Her hair is so thick and shiny. I want to love her. I want her to love me. But she hates who I am—what I am.

"Hurry. I'm getting cold. Don't do everything like a lazy girl."

"Do you want a towel for your shoulders?"

"Don't you think I would have put one on there if I wanted one? Plug in the curlers."

"Plugged in." I sit on the edge of the tub and start to comb out the back of her hair. I used to fantasize about strangling her. It's so barbaric. Even now, thinking about it makes me shiver a little. How does a thought like that live inside me? Instead, I just sit here, combing her hair.

"How was school today?"

I proceed with caution. "Good." Wait. When she doesn't say anything, I keep going. "Mr. Quinones, our art teacher, wants to see more of my drawings."

My art is a trigger for her. I know it's a trigger, yet here I am talking about it. Maybe I want her to react.

I wait.

All she says is, "Why?"

"He thinks a gallery in Chicago may be interested in taking me in as an intern."

"Uh-huh."

"He thinks I have talent. It could lead to a job." I continue to run the comb through her hair.

Her voice is soft and precise. "You do. God-given talent."

My hands shake a little. "Yes."

"We are proud of the talent God has blessed you with. We are, your father and I. We look out for you. I look out for you. You may not think I do. But I only want what's best for you."

You only want what's best for you.

She moves her head back and forth, reminding me to comb through more than one area.

For a minute, neither of us speaks. Then I say, "He thinks that I can do something with my art. Have a career with it."

"Are you sure God wants you to use what He gave you in this way? In a way that disgraces your family?"

I push. "How would this disgrace my family? This is a good thing. A really good thing."

I can see her shoulders tense and raise up slightly. My heart is racing.

"At least talk about it with Dad?"

She jerks away, turns around, and frowns at me. "You will not tell your father anything. You tricked him into letting you go to that house tonight and that pool party tomorrow."

"I didn't trick anyone into—" In a flash, she is up and now her hands are on my head. She grabs me by the hair and slams my head into the tiled wall with all her might. Pulls it back and slams it into the wall again. "God, are you testing me?" She releases her grip and I fall to the ground.

I'm holding the side of my head.

I'm lying on the bathroom floor.

She stands over me, clutching her towel. She bends over my body until her face is almost touching mine. She places her right hand on my left cheek and caresses it gently. She lowers herself down to the floor and kisses my forehead. While still pressed onto my forehead she says, almost prayer-like, in a whisper, "God has blessed you with so much. I am here as your guardian of all those blessings. I love you. So much. I will pray about your art and see what God tells me to do." In the same low, hushed voice, she continues, "You will not say anything to your father or anyone. Use the bathroom downstairs and wash yourself." She releases her lips from my skin and looks directly into my eyes. "You fell off your bike."

I am in the guest bath looking at myself in the mirror. This is when it's helpful to have this head of hair. This ridiculous hair, even with a short haircut, can camouflage the worst of clues. I feel under the hair where my head met with the tile. Bumps. I look at my fingers. A little blood, but nothing that I can't deal with. I've dealt with more. I know how to be numb. I open the medicine cabinet and grab the aspirin. Pop two into my mouth, run the sink, and stick my head under it. I take a big gulp of water. I move my whole face and head under the cold running water. It feels good. Like what just happened is being rinsed away.

"Evan? Are you downstairs?"

"Just washing up, Dad."

"I'll be in the kitchen."

He wants me to tell him. He wants something different. Right now, I'm scared of what something different will mean. I towel dry my face and hair. I mess up my hair, pushing it around, trying to do something presentable with it. I stand back and look at myself in the mirror.

I try to look casual.

I smile.

Too much teeth.

I smile with less teeth.

I practice being normal.

I run up to my room as fast as possible and close the door behind me. I take off my shirt and open my closet. What do you wear that says *everything is okay*? As I stand there sifting through my closet, it hits me for the first time that I have a uni-form. Mostly dark, long-sleeved shirts and dark jeans. No real color. Everything is black and navy. I grab a navy button-down shirt and put it on. I look at my reflection in the full-length mirror inside one of the closet doors. I should probably change the Band-Aid on my head. I peel it off. It's looking much better. Maybe no Band-Aid at all. I grab my backpack, then stop. I open the drawer that has all my books in it. I move some out of the way and grab the biggest one. Hidden inside are sheets of paper. At least a dozen drawings, all kinds, that were once part of different notebooks. I've torn these out and saved them. I look over them quickly. Can I give any of these to Mr. Q?

I like the way my dad's car smells when the windows are down. A mix of motor oil and leather. You don't smell the cigarettes as much with the wind blowing in.

"Thanks for helping with Mom's hair. It means a lot to her."

I nod but say nothing.

"What did you two talk about?"

I look straight ahead. "Just the house, mostly."

"Do you need any money for anything?"

"No. It's just dinner at the house—we're not planning on going anywhere."

"We should bring something. You should bring something. Right? Mom usually bakes something to take, but she was busy." *Busy being horrible.* "We'll stop at Geffy's and pick up dessert." He pulls into the grocery-store parking lot and parks the car. "I'll come in with you. I need to pick up butter. You can pick out whatever you think is right."

He knows.

He knows something happened in the bathroom. He's trying to make up for it. He'd probably give me his car if I asked him.

I say, "You can get something. I'll wait here. Cheesecake is always a safe bet."

"You sure?"

"Yes. If not cheesecake, then a cake. Everyone likes cake. Thanks, Dad." My heart is breaking but I know he's trying in his own fucked-up Dad way. I watch him walk away, across the parking lot. This tall, solid, handsome man who has had no backbone for so long.

I don't want to be like him. He's numb most of the time. I want to feel.

I pull my visor down and check my reflection in the mirror. I'm practicing *normal.* I smile into the mirror. What will I say to Henry? My eyes are the problem. They're usually a giveaway. I'm losing my ability to separate all the different parts of my life. I take out my phone from my backpack and text Gaige:

Just checking—u still want 2go 2party tomorrow?

I'm hoping something came up. The last thing I need right now is all these parts of my life intersecting. Why not invite my family to the pool party? Hell, let's get the pastor and church involved too. I look at myself in the mirror again. I smile. Bigger. I try to smile with my eyes, but my eyebrows keep doing some weird thing when I try it. Is my mother right? Am I that ugly? My phone starts to buzz. It's Gaige. For some reason I answer it. "Hey."

"I'm all in for tomorrow. Any chance we could do anything tonight?"

"Cool, but tonight I'm . . . I've got something."

"Damn! How late is it going? I can pick you up after. You know, maybe?"

"I can't. My parents, church stuff." What I've learned over the years is that if I ever want to get out of something all I have do is work the words *church stuff* into a sentence. It's a guarantee to instantly becoming the most undesirable person—even to other church kids.

"Uuuuuugh. You are such a cock tease. I didn't want to have to get online for . . ."

What? A kiss has turned into . . . what's this? I look out my window. "My dad's coming. I'll see you tomorrow. Okay?" I hang up and smile in my dad's direction.

The door opens and he climbs in. "Here. Take this." He hands me a bag. "I got a cheesecake and a cake. Something for everyone. There's butter in there too. Take it out and put in the backseat. I don't want to forget it."

"Thanks." Two desserts? *He knows.*

"Flip it up."

"Huh?"

"Your visor. It's down. Were you checking the hair?"

"It's short and I just . . ."

"Looks good. Was that Henry on the phone?"

I stall slightly. "Gaige." How is he so observant all of a sudden?

He pulls out of Geffy's parking lot and onto the road. "The hair's good. He did a good job. Nothing to worry about."

eighteen

"Henry?" Mrs. Kimball calls upstairs from the kitchen while Mr. Kimball passes through, bags in hand, on his way to load the car. "Evan is here."

"Be down in a minute."

Mrs. Kimball turns to me and my grocery bag. "What's all that?"

"Dessert."

"You didn't have to do that. I have brownies," Mrs. Kimball says, taking the bag from me.

"Dinner is more than enough. You shouldn't . . ."

"She didn't. I did," Mr. Kimball yells from the garage. I can hear the trunk slam and him walking around. "It's a mix, but it's a good one."

Henry comes rushing down just as Mr. Kimball walks back in. His dad says, "Evan brought groceries, apparently."

"Cake and cheesecake." Mrs. Kimball gives Henry a hug

and then Mr. Kimball is hugging him, and there's all this hugging going on. Mrs. Kimball comes over, and before I can step out of the way, her arms are around me. "Enjoy the meat loaf."

"Thank you again. It's my favorite."

"I know. You guys didn't really have summer this year. Together." Mrs. Kimball is looking at me, really looking, and suddenly it feels like the bumps on my head are growing. Like maybe I've started bleeding again and she can see it, all of it.

"Let's not make this the longest good-bye," Henry says quietly.

The Kimballs are gone in a flurry of waving hands. Henry closes the door after them and starts up the stairs. Halfway up, he stops, comes back down again and straight into the kitchen. I'm leaning on the counter. Henry pauses at the far corner of the kitchen island and exhales. Silence.

I look at him. "What?"

"I'm nervous."

"Me too." As my phone starts buzzing. It's on the counter. Before I can grab it, Henry beats me to it. He reads a text out loud:

Meant what I said earlier—I can pick u up!

Shit. "It's just. It's the thing tomorrow. You're going too and . . ." I have no idea what to say.

"Is this Gaige?"

"I wanted to see if he was planning on going. For sure. See if he had the address."

"It sounds like he's coming. Is he picking you up?" Henry takes a seat on a stool at the kitchen island and leans in toward me. I'm still motionless at the kitchen counter. Near the sink.

"He offered. I told him I was just going to ride my bike."

"Tell me about him."

"Nothing, really. He's from California."

"Where in California?"

"I'm not completely sure, but I think up north." *It's Sacramento.* For some reason I don't want him to know that I know.

"Why does he miss you? What's the deal, Evan?"

"What? He didn't text that. I don't know. We just met at camp and now he's here checking out a school. I told you all this already. That's it."

Is he jealous?

Do I like that he might be?

Henry looks down at the butcher-block top on the kitchen island and says, "I think my parents know."

"Know what?"

He looks up at me.

"Henry, what are you talking about?"

"This summer was different. Right? Not hanging out made me think about things." He laughs nervously and scratches the sides of his head. "I would go by your house almost every day."

I work hard to make the words come out calmly. "What about your parents? I mean, what do they know?"

"That I'm gay."

There it is. I'm afraid to say anything. So I don't.

"I think they know I'm gay, and what sucks is that I think they're more okay with that than maybe I am." His eyes well up. The last time I saw Henry cry was when his dog died. He wipes his nose with his hand and says, "And at the monastery . . ." He stops himself and looks at me. Like he wants me to finish the sentence.

I must be in shock, because I feel almost frozen. All I can manage is "I'm sorry." I want to go over and hug him, but I'm stuck.

He takes a breath and wipes his nose again, this time with his sleeve. "You seemed far away this year—I don't know. Claire. She's literally far away, at school. And now there's this new guy, Gaige." The tears come hard this time for a split second and then he pulls them back.

Now I can feel myself welling up and I try to move closer to him. "Hen—"

"No." He puts his hand out and stops me. He has control over his emotions again. "I know it's stupid, but Claire . . . I'm supposed to be glad she's gone away to college and not here bugging me, but I don't feel that way. She makes me feel—strong."

I never see Henry as weak. He's the one person, the one guy, who is so *sure*. So *strong*.

Henry looks right at me. "I miss you too. Gaige doesn't have a monopoly on that."

I don't know what to say to that. To all of this, really. I'm so filled with emotion right now and I'm scared as shit to feel any of it.

"I guess I'm jealous. Fuck. There it is. That's it."

"Of Gaige?"

"I want you to be the guy who held me all night. In my room when I couldn't stop crying. And at the monastery you pushed me away. That hurt." He takes a breath. "I'm also scared that I want that."

"Henry, it's not simple."

"Have you been avoiding me? Is that what camp was?"

"What about Amanda? And Ali, the girl you flirted with at Bugle's?"

"Everything isn't always clear."

"Exactly."

"Ev, you don't share anything with me. I had to find out from Jeremy about no more Greek school and you possibly doing an internship in the city? In fucking Chicago. It's like you have this whole other life. Lives! I don't think you understand that this is, or should be, a two-way friendship. I don't know how to be around you because you don't *give* me anything. I keep trying."

"What do you want me to give you?"

"You. I want you."

I look at Henry and wonder how a boy so smart can be so

clueless. "You want what almost happened at the monastery? That's not the way the world works. The world works in black and white. Neat and tidy. I get that. This—this is too fucking messy."

"Life's fucking messy." Henry's eyes are clear and sharply focused on mine.

I look away. "That doesn't work for me."

"I'm gay and I want you to be more than my tennis buddy. Is that neat and tidy, black and white enough for you?"

I suddenly shut up.

My heart's pounding so loud I feel it coming out of my ears.

Henry says, "When I kissed Amanda all those times—the times we had sex. It never felt like that one time you and I almost kissed. Fuck, you and I barely touched and I felt so—alive."

I stand there silent and in awe of this boy in front of me who is so raw, trusting, and open. This one person who has never judged me.

"You have to say something. Don't leave me out here alone and don't you dare fucking leave."

"What?"

"That's what you do. You just leave. Don't do this to me. Not now. I'm fucking putting out so much stuff and if you just pull your shit . . ."

I'm angry. Angry that he knows this about me. "Henry, maybe you don't get to have what you want right now."

"What do you want?"

I don't know. I take him in and see these brilliant, sad, and beautiful eyes that are looking at me in a way I always thought I wanted. A way I never imagined was possible, and it scares the hell out of me. And fuck, he's right. I want to leave.

Instead I say, "I'm scared."

"Me too, but also not scared."

He walks over to where I'm standing. He's now right in front of me. My skin feels tingly. He grabs the bottom of my shirt with both hands and pulls me closer to him. I stop breathing. He shifts himself even closer and starts slowly putting his hand under my shirt toward my back. I feel paralyzed, scared, thrilled. As if ice water is pumping inside my body. He leans in closer. I can feel his breath on my skin. He whispers, "Ev, I want to be the one you trust." With that he removes one of his hands from my back and places it on the back of my head. Both my hands are locked around his waist. He leans in and kisses me full, soft, hard, and without any hesitation. I kiss back. Everything about this feels like that moment when you've finally reached the top of the highest peak on a roller coaster and you've just opened your eyes.

There's always a major shift change in mood whenever I leave Henry's house and come home. This time, I feel it even more— the sense of dread that finds its way under my skin when I quietly enter our house.

It's early for both of them to be asleep. I walk quietly down the hall toward my room and pause outside my parents' bedroom door. I hold my breath and listen. Snoring. Both of them. I'm safe.

My head is still living in that kiss. It's good no one is here to see me grinning like an idiot.

I go into my room and turn on the light. I see my desk drawer open and my stomach drops. I dump my backpack and walk slowly over to my bed. On it is a neat and orderly pile of my drawings and artwork. All ripped and cut into small pieces. There's a note at the top.

The face of the Lord is against them that do evil, to cut off the remembrance of them from the earth. Psalm 34:16

nineteen

I'm pacing outside the monastery windows.

Anger is an emotion that I often feel but never want to acknowledge. Maybe it's because I'm afraid of what I'll do. That I'll be like her. That I am like her.

My pockets are filled with all the cut pieces of paper. The ones that used to be my drawings. The ones that I had wanted to give to Mr. Quinones.

There's a warm light that shines on the monastery. It won't be around much longer. Maybe a couple more weeks; then we're into the gray season.

I pace.

And pace.

I'm stalling. I don't have a plan.

What do I do about these torn drawings? About her? About Henry? Gaige?

I've worked so hard to keep everything down. To not feel pain. Not react. Blend in. But it's not working anymore. I hurt. I feel it. My body aches. My head thumps. I start to cry, sit down, and look inside the tall windows. I can see all the usual suspects of the statue party. I swear someone is moving them. I look inside and scan the faces. I sit there for a while and then I get up from the little patio and head onto the lawn. I move directly to the nearest tree and start digging along the base of the trunk. The earth on top is soft, but it gets denser as I dig. I grab a thick branch from the ground nearby and use it to dig deeper. I dig until I hit something harder than soil.

I use the branch to cut around the dark-blue metal box. It's even more rusted than the last time. I'm digging with my hands now until I can maneuver the box out and place it on my lap. It's about the size of a small microwave. I open the latch.

Inside are five notebooks. Just like the one I carry with me. They're really unremarkable, as far as journals go. Black-and-white composition notebooks with faded edges. Each one has a large, wide, blue rubber band wrapped around it vertically. On each cover, there's a text box in the center. I've debated so many times as what to write there. Nothing has ever felt like the perfect thing.

The notebooks are filled with the opposite. I've documented all the ugly moments of abuse with such careful detail in the journal entries and drawings that at first glance through all the pages, all of it looks beautiful. The penmanship is neat and perfect. The sketches and colored pencil illustrations almost mythical in style.

I lift out all five notebooks, bury the box, and shove the notebooks into my backpack. I unload all my pockets of the torn drawing paper and put those in the backpack as well. I pull off my baggy white long-sleeved shirt and drop it on top of the box. My mother bought it at the Depot because it's a shirt that won't show off my body. It will keep me covered. It will keep me good and wholesome and pure. *This is the kind of shirt you can't seduce a boy in.* I cover the shirt and the box with dirt, and then I pull out the black T-shirt I packed—the one that fits me—and change into it.

twenty

Ali's house is one of those typical ranch homes built in the eighties. Nothing about it stands out except her mom is a landscape architect and she's created front and back yards that are ridiculously awesome. They look like something out of *Alice in Wonderland* meets the Chicago Botanical Gardens. I've been here before and I walked around like a zombie. I must have asked Ali's mom a million questions about how she planned this. What was her inspiration. How long it took. The names of the plants. I was in geek overdrive.

"P-P-P-P-aaaaaaaanos!" Jeremy rushes out of the house to greet me. He's wearing bright-yellow board shorts and no shirt, and his hair is slicked back. "I've been in that pool for the last hour. Here, let me show you where you can put your bike."

"You running the show here?"

"You know me. I command a room."

"Do you?"

"You're the most requested man. Gaige. Kimball. I wish the other Kimball was here. Claire."

"She'd crush you. So, everyone's here?"

"Almost everyone."

I lean my bike in the garage and follow Jeremy into the house. The house where I'll see Henry for the first time after our kiss. I'm so nervous and excited that every step, every breath, feels cautious and deliberate.

Then the question inside the house becomes *Where do I store this backpack?*

Jeremy is asking me where my suit is or if I plan to swim in all my clothes like the good Greek boy that I am. Sometimes I very much feel like a stranger in my own town. Not that being Greek feels comfortable either.

"You know, I'm probably going to just lay low with the swimming. I may be getting a cold."

"What? No. Give me the backpack and get in the pool. You're going in one way or another, Panos."

He pulls open the door to the hall closet, grabs my backpack, throws it in. I'm watching it leave my side in slow motion. I'm reaching for it when this voice behind me says, "I was wondering when you'd show up."

Gaige.

It's either a really good thing or a really bad one that Jeremy's here right now. But then, like that, he's heading toward the French doors and back outside. "Come out here, losers! I'll be over heeeeeere!" And with that he jumps right into the pool.

Gaige has on a pair of blue-and-orange-striped loose board shorts and a white T-shirt. The look on his face makes me think either he's high or this is his "sexy" face.

I look outside. I see Henry. I wave as Gaige watches. All my senses are in overdrive. It's as if every single object and person is waving at me, demanding my attention.

"I don't think they can see us from outside. The glare. They've been asking about you. They thought I'd know where you were."

"Oh."

"Are you going to go in?"

"The pool?"

Clearly he's been in. His swim trunks are soaked and so is his hair. He's normal without trying to be. I doubt he practices in the mirror like I do.

He says, "You know, at the risk of sounding like a cliché, we should probably talk." And he smiles. It's the smile that got me at camp. The one that made me want to kiss him.

"Yep. I got that sense from your texts. The ones that said *let's talk*."

"I'm not subtle."

"Not sure that here is the right place."

"I go back tomorrow. It's going to have to be."

I can see Henry outside. He's standing with a drink in one hand and a hot dog in the other. Talking to Ali. They look good. They look like they belong together. Both tall. Blondish. She's in a teal bikini. He's in dark-emerald swim trunks with a wide, white stripe down one side, and . . . fuck! He's looking good. This is a good picture. Why would I want to interrupt this picture?

"Evan?"

"Mmmm."

"You want to keep staring at those two or can we talk?"

"Evan!" Tommy Goliski swings into our orbit.

Oh, no. "Tommy. This is—"

"We've already met. Gaige is a cool guy. It's like you're morphing in front of my very eyes, Evan."

"What?"

"There's someone in there." He pokes me in the chest. Hard. "If you can keep the queer at bay." He pokes me again. "Don't be this guy. Be . . ." He points to Gaige. "Be that guy." And with that he walks away as quickly as he circled in. If he only knew.

Gaige rolls his eyes. "What a dick."

"Sorry, Tommy thinks he—"

"Henry? Is there something?" Gaige doesn't skip a beat.

"He's my best friend and I should go say hello."

Gaige shakes his head. "Evan, this isn't hard. I'm cool with you and Henry, if that's a thing. It was fun at camp. I just thought we could have more fun. No strings attached. I'm not looking for a boyfriend. I have school to think about."

"Gaige, I'm sorry. We can't talk here. How about if after the—"

He leans in a bit and whispers, "No. I just want to get laid. How can you not get that? *Damn*. Just text me later. Don't make this into something else." He moves back and then walks out toward the pool area. What the fuck just happened?

Idiot. I'm a fucking idiot. I've been worried that I have to figure something out and what the kiss with Gaige meant, and to him it was nothing. My mind is spinning. That's what it must be like to know. To know exactly who you are. To be so sure, without angst. I feel somehow deflated, stupid, disappointed, and relieved all at the same time.

I go outside and move closer to where Henry and Ali are standing. Henry sees me. I wave. He waves and goes back to talking to Ali.

"I didn't think you'd show." This is from Tess, who's just walked up. "You want something to eat? The burgers are really good, I hear. I don't eat meat now, but—"

"Um, I'm good. Thanks."

I'm watching Henry with Ali look like they're having a good time. I'm not swimming but my head sure as hell is.

Tess leans in toward my left ear. "I want to ask you something."

I nod.

"Hey, guys, we need to see about starting a pool volleyball

thing. Right?" Jeremy swoops in, clueless as ever. He genuinely wants to play volleyball. He links his arm with Tess's and then walks up to Kris and links his other arm with hers. They're being whisked away like contestants on some game show they had no idea they were part of. As they're walking away I hear, "Panos, get your ass out here and play with us!"

Tess and Kris finally break away. "Jeremy, you're an asshole, and I don't want to play volleyball, at least not with you!" Tess heads back toward me.

Jeremy tries to shrug it off and says to no one in particular, "Let's get some volleyball started." He turns around briefly and yells in Kris's direction, "You may want to join us for this, Jorgenson. It is your area of expertise, after all."

Tess wastes no time. "Okay, now that *that's* over, let me just get—"

"She has a crush on Henry," Kris blurts out, and then looks at Tess and shrugs. "Sorry, I had to. I was afraid you were never gonna do it."

I snort-laugh a little, relieved that it's not me. Tess glares at me, then at Kris. I'm completely blown away. "What's happening?"

Tess looks right at me intently. "Okay. Here's the deal. I have had a crush on Henry since moving to this boring-ass school. You're always around him. You know him better than anyone, and now that Amanda is out of the picture . . ."

"Well, there's Ali now."

"Ali is merely a simple distraction. I can take care of that."

I say, "Listen, I gotta get out there and—participate."

Tess seems excited about this idea. "Oh, brilliant. Get out there and separate Henry from Ali. She has had him cornered since he got here."

And I go.

Just do this. Be normal.

"Henry. Ali. Thanks for inviting me. It's great. Place looks awesome."

They stare at me. She's visibly not happy about me showing up.

"Hi, Kevin."

"Evan."

"Right." She laughs. "You were the one who loved my mom's landscaping. She's over by that fountain. She *had* to be here." Ali rolls her eyes big before continuing, "My last party got a little out of hand, so now we're being chaperoned. Cute. Anyway, she'd love to talk to you more about it."

Nice. She's clearly trying to shoo me away. Henry gets the girl and I get landscaping.

"You should probably grab something to eat before all the good stuff runs out. I need another go-around myself. Be back." Henry smiles at Ali. He looks at me and motions with his head to follow him toward the kitchen.

"I didn't think you'd show up," says Henry.

"There was a moment . . ." I try to be cool, but it just comes out sounding sad.

"Really?" He sounds surprised.

"Can we go inside for a minute?"

At first I think he's going to say no, but then he says, "Okay."

Somehow we've bypassed Tess and Kris and we're standing in the middle of the most 1980s bathroom ever. There's a crazy-big whirlpool tub in the corner with two giant spotlights above it. The shower is trimmed in brass, as is the large Hollywood-style light bar above the mirror and sinks. I don't even know what I'm going to say, but everyone outside and all this back and forth—Go. Stop. Talk. Don't.—is messing with my head.

Suddenly he leans in. Hard. He puts both of his hands on the back of my head and plants an awkward, sloppy kiss on me. I push him back. I smell alcohol on his breath.

"Henry." I pull away.

He slowly pulls back and looks at me, his hands still on the back of my head.

"What?"

"I don't want to get caught. In here." Plus not like this. Not here in Ali's house. "Have you been drinking?"

He removes his hands from the back of my head and puts two fingers up to his lips. "Shhh." Then laughs.

"You have. Where's alcohol? Ali's mom is . . ."

"Shhh . . ." He leans in, trying again to kiss me. I squirm as he puts his hands on the back of my head, this time running his fingers clumsily through my hair. *Shit. He feels the bumps.* I wince and move away.

Suddenly he's focused. "Are you okay? What happened?"

"It's nothing. It's from my fall. From before." I pull away.

"Ev."

I raise my shoulders, trying to create some sort of release. Something. "I wasn't sure I'd come today, and when I decided to, I didn't know what I'd do. Say."

"Okay."

"And you're drunk."

"I'm not drunk. I just had a few drinks. I needed to loosen up."

"This isn't the right time to talk about this."

"*Fuck you!* It never is."

My eyes go wide and for a split second I'm scared. Not scared of someone hearing us in here, but scared of Henry. His face instantly goes soft before he says, "I'm sorry. I'm sorry. I didn't mean it."

He has no idea that I live with a constant fear that any kind of confrontation will lead to violence.

"I messed this up, didn't I, Ev?" He tries to get closer.

"You were right, Henry. There's so much I don't tell you."

We look at each other.

"I've got something to show you. It'll explain a lot and it'll probably make for more questions, but it's the only thing I can think of."

"Henry?" Ali's voice comes through the door. *Shit.*

"Be right out." Henry looks at me with a *What do we do now?* face. I motion for him to go out. "Just a second."

From the other side of the door: "What?"

He walks out, shutting the door behind him. I stand there listening.

"I was looking all over for you. Just wait for me. Don't run away." The door opens. As I'm standing there.

"Hi, Ali."

Her mouth drops open. "Evan?"

Henry re-enters. "We were looking for a Band-Aid." He seems perfectly sober right now.

"What?"

I quickly put my hand up to my head where the cut is practically healed. "I thought it was all better, but . . ."

"It opened right back up," Henry offers.

"I didn't want to go in the pool and bleed everywhere, so . . ."

"Why didn't you guys"—she looks at me, at Henry—"just ask me?"

"I don't know."

"You know, so stupid . . . I think I have one in my backpack." I fly out of the bathroom and head toward the entry hall.

Henry follows me. Ali's still in the bathroom. *Please let it still be there.*

I grab my backpack and dig out a small Band-Aid from the front pocket. Because of course I have one. I always have one, just in case. I tear it open and place it on my head.

"I'm going to get going."

"No need. Once Ali comes back out we can all—"

"It's only going to make things more awkward. Plus I took the day off from the deli today for this and I could still probably rush over there and grab a few hours. I need the money." I unzip my backpack and reach inside. "We can talk later. Here. Take these. For better or worse, these journals will explain a lot." I hand Henry my five notebooks. The sixth one, the one currently in play, is still in my backpack. Do I give that one over as well? He looks at me.

And then my hand is reaching into my backpack and I'm pulling out number six. If everything is going to collide I might as well go for it.

"Here." I hand him the last notebook.

"Henry?" Ali is coming. Henry bends into the closet, sticks the notebooks into his travel bag, and pulls out a towel.

He stands back up and waves the towel at her. "I forgot it." He closes the closet door and smiles at Ali. "Ready for a swim?"

"Are you leaving?" She looks at me suspiciously.

"I have to work. But it was an awesome party. Thank you."

twenty-one

Getting ready for church is always a big deal. We have to get up extra early so that we all look as pressed and perfect as possible. My dad and I have to wear a suit and tie and my mother is either in a dress or skirt-blouse-blazer combo. We look like a Greek political family about to do a press conference.

My mother enters my room. We still haven't spoken about what she did to my artwork. Apparently she said all she needed to. I feel nauseous and angry. "Let me take a look at you. Still haven't picked a tie?"

"This one." I hold up a navy tie with a graphic print of small turquoise flowers outlined in white.

"No. Here." She reaches into my top dresser drawer and pulls out a politician's tie. Stripes. Navy, Greek-flag blue, and white. "This is more appropriate."

She comes over to me, raises my shirt collar, and starts to

knot the press-conference tie around my neck. "Your father and I are happy to hear you worked yesterday." Working is the only thing that can get me out of church and other activities deemed worthy of my time. Being lazy is just as evil as being ungodly.

"But you didn't get enough time with Gaige, did you?"

My mind is reeling. What's going on?

She stands back and admires her handiwork. "Looks nice." And then: "Good clothes hide a lot of ugly." She pats my head and then runs a single finger down the bridge of my nose and stops right at the tip. "Did you see your friend Gaige?" She then puts her hands in mine, starts to hum, and leads me in a slow dance. She's smiling. I follow her lead but am completely confused. We're dancing around my room, she's still humming, and my head is throbbing. "You can pass for handsome if you try."

"Well, look at you two. Smiling, dancing, and looking good." My father enters. My mother releases my hands and twirls to show off her outfit and newly fluffed hair. "Very nice, Vee."

I can barely hear what he's saying because I'm so focused on trying to figure out what she knows.

My dad says, "You look very handsome, young man."

"That suit helps. Give us a minute, Eli." She smiles at him and he walks out.

She takes my hands again and this time slows down until we're cheek to cheek. "Did you miss your boyfriend? The one you seduced?" My hands instantly go cold. The tone in her voice doesn't change. "I showed your diary to the pastor and he told me what was in it." She pulls back and looks at me with cold, hard eyes.

"When did you? How?" My throat tightens.

"You're not the only one who can be sneaky. You forget that thing at home sometimes. I need to know what you're doing behind my back."

"It's not what you— Nothing happened."

"It's my fault. I assumed that Bible camp would be a place to be with people are are right. Good. But evil can be anywhere. It's always in you, so it doesn't matter where I put you." She sits on the edge of my bed and gently adjusts her hair with her left hand.

"Mom, it was nothing."

She's not looking at me. Her voice is steady. "I'm not sure what to do. I mean, clearly Gaige is not a boy who is of God, and you will never see him again, but I don't know."

"About?"

She lifts her head. "You." She exhales slightly, gets up, and stands in front of me. With her high heels we're almost closer to being eye to eye. She places a palm on each of my shoulders. "Pastor Kiriaditis said that it's probably a phase. He wants to talk to you after service." She flicks imaginary dust off my shoulder. "Like it will just—poof—go away."

"It was a mistake. I'll talk with him. We can pray," I offer desperately.

What else did the pastor tell her? Did he read everything? It had to have been the last journal. The others were buried. *Damn it, Evan. Remember what else was in there.*

She cradles my face with her hands. "Let's go to church. You look very handsome." With that she turns around and exits. I stand there waiting, terrified.

My dad walks in. "Sleep okay?"

Still stunned. "Sure."

"What's wrong? You're white as a wall. Sick?"

"Just my stomach."

"Probably something you ate at the pool party. We'll be down in the car."

I pull my phone out of my pocket. Nothing. Not a single text. No Gaige. Most of all, no Henry.

Sitting in church I think of all the other kids my age who come here. I only see them when we're at service. I wonder, are any of them gay? At least one.

Phase. Pastor Kiriaditis called it a phase. *Gay.* Will I ever be able to hear the word without the stigma?

Without shame?

My mother's nails dig into my left leg. She leans in to me, smiling and scanning the room to make sure no one is watching.

"Stop daydreaming." She catches someone's eye and smiles bigger and waves. "Don't embarrass me." She grabs a hymnal, motions for me to do so as well, and then we all stand. We start to sing. I roll my eyes covertly. She sings louder.

Objectively, my mother is tone deaf. So am I, but I know it. She thinks she has a beautiful singing voice. Listening to her sing is one thing, but watching her sing is a thing to behold. Like her favorite singer, Céline Dion, she sings with abandon, with closed eyes and lots of head swaying. I glance over and catch my dad's eye. He sees me, smiles, and puts his right index finger to his lips.

Once service is over, everyone starts buzzing about, and my mother turns into the most social person here.

I tell her, "I'm going to see Pastor Kiriaditis."

She nods. "Good."

"I'll meet you back up here once I'm done."

I knock on the door to the pastor's office.

"Come in. Sit down," he says from his plain wooden desk. For a church that can be big on dramatics, the décor is surprisingly sparse. It's one of the things I miss about the Greek Orthodox Church—the pomp, the circumstance, the over-the-top interiors and all the showmanship.

We look at each other, and even though I'm pissed and all I want to do is silently brood, of course I have to fill the silence.

"Everything okay, Pastor?"

"I'm not sure where to begin, Evan."

"I heard you read my journal." All of a sudden, in this room, I don't care what he thinks anymore. Let him know the truth—all of it.

"She told you?"

"This morning." My voice is firm.

"Your mother asked me to look. I didn't think it was right, but then she said she was worried about you. Worried that you are troubled and that you may try to hurt yourself, so . . ."

"I wasn't going to hurt myself, Pastor. It was her way of getting you to read it."

"I realize that now." He seems uncomfortable.

"You told her about what happened with Gaige?"

He nods. "I told her you needed prayer, like most boys your age, and that you are probably conflicted about your sexuality."

"What else?"

He goes silent.

"Pastor?"

"That's all. I said everything else in there was about school. Your future. Things like that."

"Did she ask about anything else?"

"She saw the drawings of her. The one where she's standing over you."

He looks conflicted, but not because he doesn't know what

to say but more like he doesn't know what to do. "She wanted to know if there was anything in there about her. About your relationship. I told her that there wasn't anything specific." He looks right at me when he says, "It was more general. Things most kids feel about their parents."

He lied to her. There's nothing *general* in the journals. Maybe he's more astute than I'm giving him credit for.

"Did she confess to anything?"

"There's a trust between a pastor and his—"

"You read my journal. She took it from my room. Where's that trust with me?"

He exhales. "She said that she may be hard on you sometimes but that it's only because she wants you to be a good son. A godly man." He stops for a few seconds, then adds softly, "Not a homosexual."

I can feel myself getting angry.

"Evan, I told your mother—and, I believe, the Bible tells us—that homosexuality is a sin."

"The prayers didn't change anything."

"You have to continue to pray and look to God for answers and strength."

I rub my palms on each pant leg in an attempt to dry them. Between feeling nervous, then mad, then confused, my body has decided to respond with lots of sweat. "She didn't tell you anything else? Did she tell you what our relationship is like?

Between me and her?"

"When sin is involved sometimes harsh measures are needed, and dedicated action is proper." His words come out flat.

I can feel myself getting angrier with every sentence. "Pastor. With all due respect, I don't think you understand." My phone is vibrating in my jacket pocket.

"Maybe a family conversation. All of us in the same room with the word of God." He drops his head a bit. I stare at him. My phone keeps vibrating. *Fuck*.

He looks down at his hands and says earnestly, "Evan, God can help you."

"Where's he been, then?"

He raises his head and looks at me. "He's always here. We're the ones who turn our backs."

"I've done almost everything right. Almost always." My voice is cracking. My phone vibrates again. I start to cry but quickly pull myself together. "Where is God when she beats me?" And then I start crying again. "You read that, right? I know you read that."

His eyes well up slightly as he says, "She wants you to be your best self in God. She believes you tried to lure another boy at camp."

"I didn't lure, seduce, or do anything to anyone. It was a kiss. Just a kiss." I'm sobbing now, my voice cracking. "And you told her about it. You didn't have to. You didn't . . ." I stop because the tears take over and my voice gives out.

"That's a sin. She has a right to be worried and to—"

"You read what she thinks is best for me. It's just one notebook. There are others. Filled. Filled with what she's done."

He looks at me for a second with the face of a man who actually might understand. A man who can talk about this beyond what he has been taught by his church to say. Then that second is gone and he says, "We can all pray about this together. There's healing in that."

"She's been getting away with this since I was five."

His voice gets a little shaky. "Evan, we can figure out how to handle this. I believe we all want the same thing. The best for you. The best that God can offer. We can all talk about this."

"Okay." I attempt to pull myself together even though the level of anger I'm feeling accelerates my breathing. "I know how to do this. I do this all the time. Actually, *this* is what I do. I make everything okay. I make it all normal when it's not at all." I take longer, slower breaths.

"Prayer can be very powerful."

"I'm going to be eighteen in less than two months. I can handle it."

The pastor sighs. "That isn't the right approach."

Now I'm back to mad. "No. *This*"—I gesture with my hand around the room—"isn't the right approach. You and this church are not the right approach. Even when you're faced with the truth—when it's right there in front of you in black and white—you pretend it's something else. And I'm not doing that anymore."

And I walk out.

twenty-two

Once we're back home, I run to the downstairs bathroom and close and lock the door. I haven't had a moment alone since church. On our way home in the car she kept checking on me in the backseat. Finally I take my phone out of my pocket. A bunch of texts from Henry:

When can I cu?

Tonight?

I tried calling. Know ur at church. Call when u can.

At least text me back.

I want to hurt her like she hurts u. I'm sorry. Plz call me.

There's a text from Gaige:

Heading home. If I come here 4school maybe we can hang.

There's also a text from Jeremy and a video:

Panos, ur boy is back in da game! U lft when it started

gettin goooooood! Tlk 2morrow.

What the fuck is Jeremy talking about? I click on the video. It won't load. Reception down here is stupid. I leave the guest bathroom and quietly open the door right next to it that leads into the garage. I try again. It starts to play. It's a video of Henry. There's a close-up on his face. What is he doing? The image pulls back and my heart stops and I go ice cold everywhere. It's a video of Henry making out with Ali. Like, going at it. I can hear Jeremy laughing and then a hand covers the camera, and Henry's voice says, "Shut that thing off, asshole!"

I drop and sit on the garage floor, feeling sick to my stomach. I trusted Henry with so much. I felt safe confiding in him. Maybe that's the problem. I gave him too much all at once. More than he could handle. I feel nauseous and stupid. I stand up, lean over, and throw up.

"Evan!" I can hear her from upstairs.

I get back inside and yell upstairs, "Just a minute. Bathroom." I run into the bathroom and grab a towel to clean up the mess in the garage. Then I run cold water from the bathroom faucet over the dirty towel and toss it into the washing machine on the other side of the guest bath. I turn it on.

"Evan! Hurry up."

"Coming." From the bathroom sink I splash some water on my face, take a gulp from the running tap, rinse, spit it out, and then head upstairs.

My mother is flustered. She's moving everywhere, hands

waving, barking orders at me. I move like a robot, trying to push the image of Henry and Ali out of my mind.

There's a knock at the door. My mother says, "That's probably your father, and his hands are full. Get that."

I walk to the door and open it.

At first, I think I've conjured him up. *Henry.* He says, "I know you don't like people to come over, but I'm—"

My eyes go the size of Frisbees. "You can't fucking be here."

My mother's voice: "Is that your father?"

"It's just Henry. He needs to give me something before school tomorrow. I forgot some homework at his house." I shoot an *Are you fucking kidding me?* look at him and pull the door almost closed behind me. I whisper to him, "This is the worst timing ever."

"I know." His voice sounds small.

"Asshole! We have church company coming over in less than twenty minutes. Sundays. Every Sunday. You know that."

And of course suddenly my dad is there, lifting a couple of bags of ice out of the trunk of his car and calling to us. As he comes up the walk, I say, "Henry's here to drop something off I need for school tomorrow. Mom can use your help. I'll be in soon."

"Okay. How are you, Henry?"

Henry smiles at him.

"Dad. Mom really needs help. People will be here soon."

"I get it. Calm down. Going in now." He heads into the house through the garage.

"Ev, you didn't return my texts and I tried calling. So many times."

"No. Not now."

He stops and looks at me, as if he's just seeing me. "You look so handsome in a suit." He smiles. That smile. That fucking smile.

"What? Fuck you."

"I can't say something nice? What's going on?"

"Did you say something nice before you started making out with Ali? Right after I left?"

He closes his eyes. "Ev, that's not what—"

"Jeremy sent a video. It was awesome. Thrilling, actually. I'm an idiot."

"Ev, no." He tries to get closer to me.

I step back. "What are you doing? Who are you?"

"I just freaked out. Okay?" He attempts to reach for me and I flinch. He retreats.

"There's a reason why I don't tell people things. I can't trust anyone."

"No. You can!"

"You have to leave for so many reasons. And if you read all of the stuff . . . I entrusted you with the truth . . . the guy I thought you were . . ." My voice breaks. "It doesn't matter.

Please have my notebooks for me at school tomorrow, and you owe it to me to not say anything to anyone about what you know now. You owe me at least that."

"Please, I get it. Ev, let me explain!"

"No. It's my fault. I know better." I hold myself steady. "Do. Not. Text or call me!" I close the door in his face and run up to my room as quickly as possible. I take off my suit and tie and put on a pair of jeans and my Converse Chucks.

"Evan?"

"Be right out, Dad. Changing."

"I set the table, but check to see if it needs anything else."

I fling open my door. "I'll check it right now." I head toward the dining room, my dad following behind.

"Nice to see Henry."

"Yep."

"Everything okay?"

"Where's Mom?" I scan the table.

"She's changing."

"I think we may need dessert plates. I'll get 'em."

"You should have asked Henry to stay. His family had you over for dinner the other night. We should have returned the favor with—"

"Are you kidding, Eli?" My mother enters, holding her left wrist out. He proceeds to clasp her bracelet as I'm carrying in dessert plates.

"No, it would have been nice."

"This is a good Christian crowd. The right kind. We don't need that element in our home. It's enough he sees him at school and when they do tennis." She looks over the table and then at me. "Those jeans are too tight."

"They're the only ones that aren't in the washer." I start to place the dessert plates on the table.

There's a knock at the door. She frowns at my father. "Ugh. Eli, get that." She stares at me. "Then pull your shirt out. No one needs to see all that." She moves to pull the shirt from inside my pants and I instinctively jolt away, dropping the remaining plates on the floor. The crash happens quickly, but I see it as if it's happening in slow motion. I turn to look at her. Her face is calm and she smiles at me. I can hear my father down by the front door. "Welcome. Welcome." She turns away from me and heads for the door. "Thank you so much for coming. Don't you all look wonderful."

The evening is our version of dinner theater, except there are no mistakes. Everyone remembers their lines and hits their marks. Once dinner is done and every guest is escorted graciously to the front door, I help my mother clean up. She looks at me as I'm gathering dishes from the table and says, "Honey. You look so nice tonight." She strokes the left side of my face. "Thank you for being so good this evening."

I'm not sure what was different, but I say, "You're welcome," as I continue clearing the table. My dad's outside having a cigarette.

"You're so much like me. We love beauty and understand its power. It's why you draw and make your room nice." She's wrapping the leftovers individually and making a precise cluster out of all of them. All grouped together, they look like a little town. "I want you to know that I appreciate that. I see that. You're special." She puts down the dish she's working on and comes over to where I'm standing and hugs me. She must still be processing my kiss with Gaige. Maybe this is a new technique, and it's completely freaking me out.

"Mom, I don't feel very good. Is it okay if I go lie down?"

"Go. Do you want me to make you some chamomile tea?"

"No. I just need to sleep."

"Okay. Night, honey, and thank you again for tonight."

This behavior scares the shit out of me. I close the door behind me and grab some paper and a pencil and get into bed.

Three months later

twenty-three

Sometimes everything moves so slowly that it can feel like getting through one day lasts a year. The past couple of months have been the opposite of that.

Our house sold in an instant, once it was put on the market. We're now in an apartment across the lake. The Lakebridge Terrace Apartments in the Lakebridge Estates. There is nothing estate- or terrace-like about any of it. It's tract homes where every third house looks exactly the same and there are five different floor plans and exteriors to choose from. All with names like Woodbury, Castle Glen, Montague, Burling Crest, and Fawn Meadow. A made-up English-sounding community that has a 7-Eleven and a Pizza Box as its anchors in the community strip mall.

Halloween has come and gone, and we're gearing up for Thanksgiving. My birthday was the usual awkward family celebration. According to my parents, now that I'm a "man," and due to our dwindling finances, I work at the deli on the week-ends and on Tuesday, Thursday, and Friday after school. I can occasionally pick up extra hours on Monday and Wednesday. I don't mind. I like working. I managed to save $1,000 and was planning on using it to purchase a 1994 Toyota Tercel two-door coupe manual four-speed in light blue. The body's in good shape with just a few scratches. The driver's seat has a very long, clean cut on it that was "fixed" with duct tape. It's still on display at Dick's Used Cars and Trucks on Wolf Road, the main street that runs right outside our subdivision.

But my mother found the money. She made me give it to her. For bills, she said. I thought about telling my dad, but there was a part of me that felt good about it. Not about keeping it from him, but for contributing in some way.

According to my mother: *I don't need a car. Where would I go?*

I have my journals back and now they're all (but one) re-buried near the monastery.

I avoid Henry, even though I haven't been able to erase the memory, the feeling of that first kiss—no matter how much I've tried.

I've been drawing more than ever.

I go to church on Sunday.

But after that day with the pastor, it's like the truth scared him. He and my mother don't speak as often. Maybe he feels guilty. He should. I'm not sure he knows how to talk to either of us anymore. So he avoids us instead.

Gaige only texted me three more times and I didn't respond. He stopped.

Everything is back to how it was.

And I'm finally eighteen.

twenty-four

One of my favorite things about working at a deli is making sandwiches. I have my own personal way I love to create a sandwich, but customers usually have very specific ideas about what they want. I have no problem with that because the best part of all is watching people bite into something they enjoy. Like eyes-roll-in-the-back-of-their-head enjoy. To know that I did that—made something that someone really loves—is a pretty awesome feeling. And it makes me think I may not be such a bad person after all.

Today is Sunday and I get to be here all day, which I like. Usually it's a church marathon day for us, but there's one thing my parents understand better than church, and that's work. The deli closes early on Sundays, and after I've cleaned up I can go home and be alone.

Mr. Lowell owns the deli. He was a customer at the 7-Eleven in our subdivision when I used to work there. He came in almost every day and one day he asked me if I liked working there. I told him it was okay, but that I wanted something with more hours, more money, and more to do. He offered me a job.

"Evan, check the inventory to see that we have enough ham and all the cheeses for next week. It's entertaining season. We're going to be getting orders for party platters."

"Going right now."

I start toward the walk-in locker. Before I enter, I hear, "Excuse me, is Evan Panos here?"

I don't turn around. I recognize the voice and instantly start to feel warm and queasy. I quickly dive into the locker. It's cold, but I don't mind. I like it in here. I make a game out of taking inventory. I pretend that I've been captured by a rival spy agency, because I'm a spy now, and I have a plan to escape from this locker they have placed me in. I have just a few minutes (usually three) to find my way out and steal their agency secrets . . . which are hidden in the meats and cheeses.

The door to the locker opens.

It's Mr. Lowell.

"Henry is here for you. How's the inventory?"

"It looks like we can use three more hams and probably at least two more blocks of cheddar. The rest we'll be good with. But I want to take a second look. Tell him I'm busy and he can go. He doesn't have to wait." I lie, "I'll call him later."

I go back to taking visual inventory of the roasted turkey, the provolone, the salami. I hear the door close behind me. I stay in there for as long as I can stand it.

I come out and announce, "Yep, looks like we're all good except for the ham and cheddar." I scan the place and it's Henry-free. We close in five minutes, so I should be safe.

Once outside, I'm reminded how much I love fall. I try to walk when I can in order to take in the light, sky, and leaves. Plus it's just the right amount of chill and sun. I don't have to deal with a heavy coat and all the other stuff you need to keep track of. I can smell wood burning. Maybe I'll stop at the 7-Eleven and get a drumstick.

As I make my turn onto Wolf Road toward the subdivision, I hear a car slow down and pull up behind me. It stops.

I glance over. Glance away.

"Evan."

I stop, trying to tamp down the thrill I feel. I'm disappointed that he still has this effect on me. I slowly turn around. "Henry."

"Didn't mean to freak you out." He gets out and walks toward me.

"What are you doing here?"

"I'm stalking you."

"Fuck you."

Henry's eyes are not meeting mine as he says, "I'm an asshole."

"Go on." He can be difficult to resist, so I keep my distance.

"I miss you."

"Really?" I'm still pissed and if it comes out sarcastically— good.

"No. Really." He starts to move closer.

"*No.* Stop right there. You can't get any closer."

He nods. "Claire is really pissed at me. She thinks I messed up big-time and I did. Mom and Dad too."

"You told them about us?"

"Ev, this feels like I'm losing something, someone."

"Well, you are. Maybe you already have."

"Paaaaaaaaannnnooooooooos!"

Fucking Jeremy. He either has the world's best timing or the worst. In this moment I can't tell which. I hear the sound of bike tires rushing on the rocky pavement.

"Kimbaaaaaall!"

Jeremy swooshes past me so fast I almost get knocked to the ground by the sheer force of his speed. He punches his brakes and skids, for what seems like forever, until stopping and then whipping around to look at me, then Henry. He's about fifty yards ahead of where we're standing. I'm still trying to figure out if I'm completely annoyed with Jeremy right now for interrupting, or maybe relieved.

I yell, "What the hell are you doing? You almost ran right into us!"

He starts pedaling back toward me at a normal speed and waves at us. Even from this distance, I can see his big, dumb grin. I'm shaking my head and giving him one of those ridiculous looks that instantly make me seem like his disapproving father, not his friend. At times, I do feel like I'm an old man trapped in this teenager's body.

Jeremy's next to us. "Panos!" He looks over my shoulder. "Mr. Kimball." He feigns some sort of bow. "You coming from work, Panos, or are you two on a romantic afternoon stroll?" If only he understood the irony of his words.

I say, "What are you up to, besides trying to run over people?"

He gets off his bike. "Just out for a ride. I was bored. You've been working a lot lately." He looks over at Henry again. Henry attempts a smile, but it does very little to hide his unhappy eyes. "Seriously, what are you doing here, Kimball? Slumming with the working class?"

"Nothing. Just ran into Evan on my way—"

"Fuck." Jeremy makes a scrunched-up face.

"What?"

"Damn, Panos, you smell like ham." He exhales hard.

I breathe in hard. "I don't smell it."

"Congratulations, Panos, you've turned into even more of an antisocial animal. The smell isn't going to help."

"What are you talking about?"

"Kimball here keeps asking about you. You're avoiding him at school, but I told him that he shouldn't feel that special 'cause you're avoiding everyone." He scrunches his face again. "Dude! Do you rub the ham on you? You smell like shit. Ham shit."

Henry is shifting a little as he stands there. Now he's rubbing his neck and staring at the ground. I'm almost starting to feel bad for him. Almost.

"It's probably all the cheeses as well. I rub those on me too." I move closer toward Jeremy. "Here, you want a better whiff?"

He steps back so fast he almost falls. "What the fuck is wrong with you?" He shakes his head, looks over at Henry, then peers back at me before changing the subject in superfast Jeremy time. "You know I think Kimball here—whatever." Jeremy turns back to Henry. "It's no secret we've never been close. But it's not like we hate each other."

Henry doesn't say anything.

Jeremy's back to me. "What's wrong, did you guys have a lovers' quarrel? Did you upset your boyfriend?" Jeremy says in a high girl's voice.

"You're not funny. You're a moron."

"You know what?" Henry walks closer, over to me. He's a few inches from my face. "I want us to be friends again. Like before." He stares right at me as if we're alone. What does he mean, *Like before?* Before he made out with Ali? Before I let him in? Just pals? "I'm late. Ev, I'd like to talk." He glances at Jeremy. Actually stares at him like he's trying to make him disappear. When he doesn't, Henry sighs. "Later, Ev?"

"Later."

Jeremy is silent. Mouth open.

Henry turns around and gets in his car. And drives away.

I try to break the awkward silence. "Jeremy, I didn't mean it."

He snaps back to being himself. "Good. Talking later is good. You crazy kids can work it out. Oh, and Tess. *Is. Fucking. Over.*" Jeremy is emphatically making an X with his hands. "Fucking. Over!"

I don't always appreciate how self-centered Jeremy can be, but in moments like these . . . it comes in handy.

"Over how?" Jeremy and I start walking.

"I guess you can't call it *over* since it never really started, but she apparently is into someone else. Whatever. Just basic shit." He throws these words away like they mean nothing. "So what's the deal? Are you gonna be a working man from now on?"

"I can use the money." I see the 7-Eleven. We're getting closer.

"You know I was kidding about Kimball being your boyfriend, right?"

And we're back. "Yeah."

"'Cause there's a rumor going around school that he's gay. Now, I don't believe it, 'cause that dude has some serious skills with the ladies and I know he was banging Amanda, and Ali was . . ." He lowers his voice and stops walking his bike. "Pubes, the only reason I bring this up is because the rumor is that he's gay and that he's gay for you."

Oh fuck. I feel like the wind just got knocked out of me.

"Where did you . . ."

"Tommy. Oh, and Ali said that she caught you guys in her parents' bathroom. She thought you were making moves on—"

"This is crazy." I try to remain casual.

"That's what I said. If you were gay, I'd know. We've been friends forever, and man, if you were into dudes, you would have made a move on this"—he motions to his whole body with his right hand—"pure hunk of ham sandwich."

"You think if I was gay I'd be into you?"

"Simple math. You'd be gay plus I'm this guy equals of course."

"Gay guys aren't attracted to every man they see."

"You couldn't resist. Don't worry about it. I shut that shit down." Jeremy's totally oblivious.

I shake my head and say, "I'm going to the 7-Eleven to get a drumstick. Want one?"

"All your cash burning a hole in your pocket?"

"Want one or not?"

"Nah thanks, I have to go 'cause my parents are taking us out for dinner and I have to take a shower." He gets back on his bike and pauses. "Were you and Henry in the bathroom alone?"

"We were looking for a Band-Aid for my head."

"Of course. That makes sense. You're a walking accident." He starts to ride off. "See you tomorrow."

twenty-five

My room at the apartment doesn't have the same feel as at the house. I can't paint, wallpaper, or do anything too permanent here. Luckily all my bookcases fit and I can tape my artwork—what my mother has approved—on my walls, which makes the sterile space feel enclosed and safe.

Almost.

The drumstick wasn't enough, so I head to the kitchen to see what's there and go to my favorite staple, the pasta cabinet. Most homes have some pasta—we have a whole cabinet in the kitchen. Three shelves full, front to back, top to bottom. So much that if you remove a single package or box, inevitably the rest will come crashing down. There are all kinds, from your basic Kraft mac and cheese to a generic brand to some very odd-colored pasta my mom got for free from the Depot because they were going to throw it out.

I put a pot of water on to boil and notice that there's a piece of yellow cake with chocolate frosting on the counter. Just a single piece. It's on a small, round paper plate. The plate and cake are loosely covered in plastic wrap. I want to eat it so badly, but this isn't something my mother baked. It was brought over by someone. I can tell, probably a store-bought mix. This would never be an option in our home. I once snuck in a Duncan Hines Classic Yellow Cake Mix. It was contraband. I had tasted some at a neighbor's house and flipped out. I knew better than to ask for it, so I bought it one day at Geffy's Market on my way back home from school. I waited till everyone went to bed and made the cake. Not realizing that the frosting was not in the same box, I just made the cake. I hadn't bought frosting. I washed and dried all the evidence and ate the whole unfrosted yellow cake in my room.

If I eat it, this one in front of me right now, it could become a "thing," and no cake is worth that. I turn away from it and look in the fridge. There must be something to snack on while I'm waiting for the water to boil. There's a saucepan on the second shelf of the fridge. I open it and see that it's lentils. There are always lentils in this house. I have a spoonful to tide me over. Ugh. Stupid lentils.

"We're home!" My dad turns on the entry light.

"I'm in the kitchen waiting for water to boil."

"Get your coat. Your father is taking us to N-Joy Suey! We

have things to celebrate!" My mother sounds giddy and her voice is higher than normal.

I'm immediately on guard.

We walk into N-Joy and get seated near the window right away. The place is usually busy on a Sunday for dinner, but it's still early. I take off my coat and place it next to me in the booth. My father takes his off and hands it to me across the table. "Put mine there too."

My mother keeps hers on. She's always cold. Her coat is camel colored, fitted, and well tailored with a large, white, fully fake-fur collar. It's one of her favorite and most expensive pieces of clothing. She's incredibly proud of it and the way she looks wearing it. She paid almost two hundred dollars for it, on sale, at Linderfield's—not the one downtown, but the mall one. She's rubbing her hands together and blowing on them.

"It's not that cold yet, Mom."

"You don't know cold. You're young. Your blood is boiling. When I was your age I would spend all winter in a thin dress and sometimes no shoes and not feel the cold."

"We didn't exactly get snow in Greece," my dad replies, so low we can barely hear him. He takes a sip of his water as soon as the waiter sets it down, and buries his face in the menu.

"I was filled with life!" My mom makes a fist and tightens her lips as she raises her hand to the sky. I bury my own face in the menu.

"Strong and hardworking. Not like today. Everyone is just looking, always looking, at the phones and machines with dead eyes. I see you kids walking around like mindless robots staring down. What future—"

"What's the good news?" I interrupt, genuinely curious, because there's rarely any good news and I want her to stop talking.

"You tell him, Elias." She takes her hand and rubs the back of his neck.

They are rarely loving or playful with each other. My dad tries more than my mom, and it's not like I like it when I see it.

"The brothers and sisters at the church want to help me open a restaurant!" They are both smiling and looking as happy as . . . well, I don't know when the last time was that I've seen this.

The waiter comes back to the table. "Everybody ready?"

We haven't even looked at the menu, but there's no need. We always get the same things.

My mom starts to order. "I'll have the shrimp chop suey and the vegetable eggrolls, two, and just a water with lemon, please. Thank you." She hands the menu to the waiter and smiles warmly at him.

He smiles back. My dad starts to order and I glance out the window.

Holy. Shit.

Henry and his family are getting out of their car. Henry.

His parents. Even Claire is there. All of them. *Where are they going? Maybe the pizzeria? Maybe even a family outing to the 7-Eleven. Sunday-night family Slurpees? Please let it be one of these.*

But no. They are coming into the N-Joy.

"Hey, daydreamer! The man is waiting for you." My mother's eyes are now squinting directly at me.

"Oh, um. Sorry, I'll have the orange chicken," I say, trying not to stare at the *entire* Kimball family as they enter the restaurant. As they slide into a booth. Was this calculated?

My father says, "I ordered the Double Happiness for the table as well."

You could not have ordered enough happiness, I almost say. My stomach is so tense that the thought of eating seems impossible. And then Henry spots us and lights up. I force myself to smile and wave back, too late to pretend that I don't see him. It wouldn't help anyway. He'd still come over here and just be Henry.

Mom turns around and sees the Kimball family. She smiles and waves. Then she turns back around at us, scowls, and rolls her eyes. Suddenly everyone is waving. The Kimballs. Us. This is one of those moments you think can't get any worse, but it does. Henry breaks away from the pack and heads toward our table. He's taking off his coat as he approaches us, and of course he's wearing shorts. He has on a pale-blue polo shirt that makes his eyes look even brighter.

"Hi, Mr. and Mrs. Panos. So great to see you here." He smiles so large, mostly at me and my father, it's like he's trying to psych us out or something. I slowly push my coat and my dad's farther out into the booth next to me. I even try to fluff them up so the booth looks extra full.

Henry turns his gaze toward me. "Hi, Ev." He tones down his smile to something that feels more tender. "Look at this. It's later."

I try to remain incredibly casual. As if I haven't just seen him a couple of hours earlier. As if I'm not going full-on red in the face. "Hey."

"Well, it's so great to see you all here." He looks back at his family.

His mother and father are studying their menus. Claire is fixed on our table and her brother.

"I better get back to my table. Everyone is really hungry. Evan, let's get ice cream after. Okay? You can come back with us, if that's okay, Mr. and Mrs. Panos. I'll bring him home early. We both have school tomorrow and—"

"Henry, I don't think—" my mother cuts him off.

Then my dad interrupts. "Just not too late, Henry."

Henry gives me a last meaningful look and returns to his table. I want to shout, *What about my say? Can you please not decide stuff for me? Did you see how he did this . . . demanded we get ice cream? Didn't even ask!* I should have said something. I *should* say something.

"Elias! On a Sunday night you let him go with that String Bean Boy?" Even her whispers are loud.

"He's been at work all weekend. Let him have some fun." My dad is clearly in a great mood. "Henry's a nice boy and they're a good family. His sister is going to a very fancy school, right, Evan?"

"What church do they go to again?"

"His sister is going to Brown University. It's a very good school and they're Presbyterian. They go to Kalakee First Presbyterian, I think." I answer like a machine.

"That's not a real church. They believe in the gays and other sins. It's just for people to feel good. Feel-good church is not a church." She believes you should feel 100 percent persecuted at all times in order to be a child of God. "At least the girl seems to have her head on straight. And who wears shorts in winter?" She looks at me as if this is my fault.

I don't even have the opportunity to answer, or remind her that she just told me that *I don't know cold*. So much wrong here.

"You should hang out with the girl. She's pretty. Very pretty, even though she's not Greek and Presbyterian. Needs some more food on her bones." She looks at me again. "You like them like that? Skinny?"

"Mom." I try to stop this avalanche. "So what is this about the restaurant?"

The waiter and a back waiter are now at our table with

lots of plates. They start to lay them all out in front of us and I glance over at the Kimball table. Henry is looking over in this direction. Has he been looking over here the whole time? What is he thinking? He's hurt? Does he think that reading my journals makes him some sort of savior, or hero? *Do you think you can save me, Henry Luther Kimball? Think again. God couldn't save me and I asked him. A lot!*

I look back at our table, which is now covered. Every square inch of it is taken up by either empty plates or plates of steaming, hot, greasy deliciousness.

"Your father and I are going to open a restaurant. Tula and her husband, as well as Andy and his wife, Melina, are going to invest in your father and help him open up a small place. He has a great reputation." She looks at him lovingly and rubs the back of his neck again as she scoops a big spoonful of shrimp chop suey onto her plate. "Here, you want some?" She motions toward me.

I take a plate and put a little on it.

This is my mother at her best. I tell myself to enjoy it, but I can't.

My dad has already filled his plate with a little bit from every dish. Between bites he says, "I think we can get something going after the holidays. Now is not the time to start looking, but this is it. We can control our future. I've been wanting to do this for years." He keeps eating.

How can they eat?

"You know your father works very hard. Now it will be for us, not to make money for other, ungrateful people. We can work in there like a family and build something together. You can have this thing we build when we die."

I don't say anything. We've had hundreds of these discussions before. I don't want to work in the restaurant business. I don't want to inherit one. I don't want anything from either of them. We finish our meal in silence.

twenty-six

I say good-bye to my parents and they remind me to be home at a decent hour. No one mentions a time.

I walk to the Kimballs' car with them.

"There should be enough room for all of you back there." Mr. Kimball is unlocking the car and Claire gives me a hug.

It's a Subaru Outback, a new one. It has a silvery tan exterior with matching leather seats. They're a Subaru family, except for Claire. She drives a vintage BMW 2002 she inherited from her grandmother. Since I'm the shortest of the three backseat fillers, I get the middle.

"We haven't seen you in such a long time, Evan." Mrs. Kimball twists her body from the front seat in order to look back at us. She has her right hand on her husband's arm while he drives.

"I've been busy. I'm working five days a week now and sometimes even seven, if I can get the hours." I say this to my lap.

Mr. Kimball says, "Wow. Is that okay?" I glance up and

Mr. Kimball catches my eye in the rearview mirror.

"It's really nice to see you, Evan." Claire bumps into me as she says that.

"Thanks. You too. Here on a break?"

"Yep. You picked out a college yet?" Claire sounds concerned.

"Art Institute."

"Did you get in?"

"I did." That's a lie. I didn't even apply. There's no money for it.

"Awesome."

Mrs. Kimball in her always-positive way wants to know, "Are you going to study fine art, painting?"

"I think. I'm not a hundred percent sure yet."

"He's really good," Henry adds. "Can't believe you guys have never seen any of his stuff all these years."

"It's no big deal."

Mr. Kimball says, "Where are you guys going to go? There's nothing out there that's open. Do you just want us to stop at the store on the way home and pick stuff up?" He's now looking at Henry from the rearview mirror.

"Let them go out," Mrs. Kimball says. "It'll be nice to get some fresh air."

"Maybe the IHOP? It's open twenty-four hours, right?"

Henry is sitting on my left. He slides his right hand and places it just under my left thigh. *Is this what friends do?* He holds it there before chiming in, "We'll figure something out."

As timing would have it, we just pass the monastery. I instinctively look over at Henry and instantly regret doing so. His hand is still under my thigh. He turns in my direction and smiles. I'm pissed that his smile can make me feel like I'll be okay. I don't know if I can trust that. *Damn you, Henry. You can't save me.* Mrs. Kimball turns around again. "You know, maybe it is a good idea to pick up some dessert from the store."

She glances down. Notices where Henry's hand is. Henry is looking out the window now like it's no big deal. "That could be cool." He seems completely unaware that his mother is looking at us.

She smiles politely. I can't tell what kind of smile it is. She turns around and says, "You boys can always go out for a drive or whatever after."

"Sounds good." Henry looks at me. "Maybe we can make a sundae bar."

What the hell is he talking about? This is the guy of the single-flavor ice cream. No nuts, no cherry, no sauce. Sundae bar? I feel like everyone's having a conversation without me and I'm annoyed at myself for allowing it to get this far. I try to move my legs and body, but the more I do, the more Henry moves his hand under my leg. It's so uncomfortable. And maybe even a little bit of a turn-on, and that just makes me even *more* uncomfortable.

Claire says, "Maybe I'll go over to Nate's."

"Is he home? I thought he was 'never leaving NYU.'" Her mother uses air quotes but is looking straight ahead.

"He's back. At least, he'd better be."

After all the lunches and dinners I've had at the Kimball home, you'd think I'd be completely comfortable with their banter. But I still find it difficult to understand how no one ever yells or says ugly things to one another. We can't go a day in the Panos house without something being hurled at someone, physically or verbally.

Claire and her mom are talking until Mr. Kimball makes a too-quick turn into the parking lot of Fresh Fred's, and we all brace ourselves.

"Damn. Sorry. Got a little lost there for a minute." He maneuvers the car into a parking spot, almost taking out a couple of shoppers in the crosswalk. Mrs. Kimball pulls out a credit card, swivels around in her seat, and hands it to me. I just stare at it.

"Here. You and Henry are in charge of supplies."

Henry takes the credit card from his mother.

"Thanks, Mom."

Henry's heading toward the store and turns around to make sure I'm following.

Once inside, he turns to me. "Please don't go missing on me again." His demeanor has completely changed. He looks fragile, scared. "You can't keep doing that. I know I fucked up, but please don't take me for granted."

I shake my head. "Okay, but I'm having a difficult time trusting anyone right now."

Once inside the Kimball house, everyone scatters while Henry and I head into the kitchen. I'm whispering, "You know your mother saw your hand?"

Henry puts the grocery bags on the kitchen counter and looks at me. "Get the bowls."

"Seriously, we're just going to pretend that this is some kind of—"

"I don't care who saw. The last time I saw you, really saw you, was weeks ago, and I don't want to go through that again."

"They're right upstairs. You see me in school. Lower your voice." I'm shaking and sweating. I can't see myself right now, but I can guarantee this is not a good look. My hair is probably beginning to frizz and I just know my face is red.

Henry looks completely calm. "You avoid me in school. *I'm gay*. My sister knows. My parents know. You know."

I just stare at him for a second. "Amanda Hester all last year." I lower my voice even further. "You told me you had sex with her. And let's not forget Ali or the fact that I'm so fucking pissed at you."

Who am I trying to convince here? What is he saying? In Ali's house, what was that? How can he just—say it?

"Get the bowls, Ev. The ice cream is going to melt."

I know where everything is in this kitchen. I've made Greek

chicken with lemon potatoes in here. There's a large island and stools on one side. The rest of the kitchen wraps in an inverted U shape around the island. The whole space opens into a large and comfortably worn family room. But suddenly, I have no idea where the fucking bowls are.

"Ev, are you okay?"

"How can you just say that?"

"What?"

"*I'm gay*. Like you're so sure. Recent events prove otherwise."

Henry grabs five bowls from a cabinet and places them on the island countertop. "Because I am. I didn't feel anything for the girls I was with that even comes close to the way you make me feel. I'm gay."

"Are we heating the fudge sauce?" I ask, still annoyed.

"No question." Henry places all the ice cream on the kitchen island. For someone who doesn't care for sauce, he knows how sundaes should be prepared.

"You're on your own, kids." Claire strides into the kitchen, looking pretty as she always does. The kind of girl my mother would love for me to date. She hugs Henry from behind and squeezes him as hard as she can.

Henry escapes her grasp. "Ugh! Save it for Nate."

I look at her. At Henry. At the way he shakes the hair out of his eyes. At the way he's smiling at his sister, with all this love.

Claire looks at me. "I'm really glad you're here." She walks over to where I am and kisses my cheek. "See you later." And then she's off.

Henry fills a saucepan with water and places it on the stovetop.

"This is all bizarro world." I open a drawer and pull out the ice cream scoop. Henry lowers the jar of fudge into the saucepan on the stove.

"Can you hand me one of those bowls? I'm going to put the chopped nuts in there."

"Here." I hand him what was to be Claire's bowl and start in. "Aren't you nervous? How are you so sure this time? We've never ever talked about this. Didn't you have fun with Amanda? With Ali? Maybe they weren't the girls you were supposed to be with. You can't just know, just like that."

Henry looks into my eyes. "What happened with Ali—it's not an excuse, but I was confused, freaked out, a little drunk, and I wanted to be needed. I wanted someone to want me. I wanted you to, but—there. Are you happy?"

I shake my head. "So it's my fault? Don't you dare. You were drunk and you totally betrayed my trust."

"It's not like that. I wanted—want you to be sure about me. It wasn't real with Ali. I was so stupid. I drank too much."

I'm taking the lids off the ice cream containers. The tops are just starting to melt and get soft, the perfect consistency for scooping. For some reason, maybe nerves, I start to fan the top of the ice cream with my hands.

"We didn't have sex," he says as I try to keep my face neutral. "Ali and I just made out. Things got a little sloppy, but no sex."

"*We made out. We didn't have sex.* Is it all the same to you?"

"Ev, what happened between you and me was more real to me than any kiss, anything, I've ever had." He notices me fanning the ice cream. "What is this?" He starts laughing.

I instantly realize what I'm doing and stop. I place both hands on the island counter and look across it in Henry's direction. He's at the stove checking the hot fudge.

I whisper, "Okay. I felt something. I'll give you that, but how can you know anything? I don't trust you."

Henry looks back at me. He starts to walk over to the other side of the island. My side. Damn, it's a long walk. My heart suddenly seems like it may not be strong enough to take this in, and my whole body is now beyond sweating. He kisses me. Softly. I don't kiss back. He continues as he tries to place his hands into mine. I resist a little but then slowly open my palms. Our fingers intertwine and I begin to kiss him back. A little. He leans back, our hands still clasped together, and looks right at me and says, "I'm going to do everything I can to earn back your trust."

I take a gulp of air. "We should check the sauce." And what if his parents had walked in? It didn't even cross my mind during that kiss. I look at him and say, "I want to believe you."

"You can." He steps away and heads toward the stove. "The hot fudge looks ready."

From behind me I hear, "This is the slowest service ever."

I'm jolted back into reality.

"Oh man, I didn't mean to startle you." It's Mr. Kimball.

Damn, that was close.

Henry hands his parents their sundaes. "Here you go, guys, two classics. One with and one without nuts."

"You guys want to join us? We can order a movie if you want," Mr. Kimball says.

"Thanks, but I think we're going to hang out a little before I have to take Evan home."

We walk into Henry's room. He closes the door behind us, puts his bowl down on his desk, and before I can speak, think, he kisses me again. I take a few steps back and say, "Your parents."

"It's okay."

"Henry?" I do want to kiss him. Oh man, I really do. The way he looks at me right now. This is the stuff you see in the movies and think how fucking corny it is, but when it happens to you—no words are flowery enough to capture that feeling.

"Henry. You read my journals, right?"

He nods as he pulls me closer. "I'm so sorry. Between what happened at the party with Ali and not being able to explain, and then reading all that stuff, your drawings . . ."

"I've never shared this stuff with anyone. My life has been

about making sure I could keep everything separate. Keep it contained. This. Us. It disrupts that. I have to be able to trust you. Now more than ever."

"I promise you." He's looking right at me. "Nothing is worth hurting you."

I know it's only a few seconds, but this moment . . . this silent moment is my world.

"Ev, I've seen marks on your neck. Arms. Legs. A few times on your face. I didn't want to believe."

"I didn't want you—or anyone—to. It would have only made it more difficult for me."

"There were a lot of tough things to read, to see them there on a page and know you wrote them. But the hardest for me was reading about you wanting to die." He puts both hands around my waist. "Do you still feel like that?"

I don't say anything. I'm embarrassed. I fear that Henry will see me as weak. As someone who won't fight for himself, so how could he ever for fight for anyone else?

"I need you. I want you around."

I'm still quiet.

"Do you still think about dying?"

"Not anymore. I dream of escaping." *But not escaping you,* I want to say but don't.

"Was Gaige . . ."

"He was my first kiss."

"There were so many drawings of me in your journals. I

didn't see any of Gaige. . . ." He looks at me questioningly.

"Don't be a self-centered prick. I've known you longer."

He kisses me again. He moves to my neck and one of his hands goes toward my back. I can feel his fingers run up and down my spine. His other hand is moving up my leg. I push myself further into him, even though it seems physically impossible to be any closer.

"Oh man . . ." I sound as if I've been drugged, but I don't stop. He continues to kiss my neck and then starts to move back to my mouth.

"We can't," I say quickly. "I've never had sex."

Ugh. What a completely unsexy thing to say. I pull away and try to catch my breath. "Sorry."

"Don't. Look at me." Henry's hands are now on my shoulders. "You don't have to tell me or do anything more right now. I just don't want to lose you. Again."

The person who was supposed to love me the hardest—the most unconditionally—has always wanted me gone. No matter how hard I tried to be perfect. Now, this boy—who knows all my imperfections and has seen all my hurt laid bare—wants me to stay.

twenty-seven

I'm pretty useless today.

Being at school the day after my evening with Henry is really just an exercise in finding new ways to pretend to be paying attention. I'm not exactly nailing it.

"Mr. Ludecker, I can hear you."

"Sorry, Mr. Q."

Jeremy turns to face me and mouths something. I shrug. He mouths again. Nothing. He writes on the edge of his drawing paper, *You have to do this for me!* I shake my head no. Jeremy rolls his eyes.

"Evan, can I see you for a minute?"

"Sorry, man." Jeremy actually looks genuinely sorry.

I walk over to Mr. Quinones. "Do you have anything for me now?" he asks.

I've been hoping he'd forget about it. "I know I've asked for an extension . . ."

"Are you still interested in the internship?"

I don't know how to answer.

"Your work from class is good; I was hoping to—"

I look at the floor and say, "It's not a good idea. The internship isn't really for me."

Blank. Just an empty stare back that makes Mr. Q's face look like someone shut him off.

Hoping to make this better, I offer, "Maybe once I graduate. If the program is still available and art is something I—"

"You're not interested?" I can tell he doesn't believe me.

"Evan"—the switch is back on—"you don't have to do this. Any of it. All this stuff, art and—it's your decision. The internship isn't a commitment for life. I think it's a good way to figure out what you don't want."

He's right. Every choice, every decision seems so important to me. Maybe it could feel good to take on something, make a choice, as if it's okay for it not to be perfect. I nod and say, "I'll think about it."

"Good."

I stand in line to get my lunch and notice Henry and Jeremy already sitting down. Henry smiles and Jeremy motions me over. I nod and wave, trying to seem ordinary, just in case anyone is staring and can tell just by looking at me that I've changed. That Henry and I are different.

Lunchtime isn't always a welcome break for me. The

cafeteria is a social place, and stories get shared and rumors are born. Keeping a low profile has been a fairly good strategy, but the last few months I've had a bit more attention than I'm comfortable with. And after the very, very recent events, I'm super nervous about not just my worlds colliding but my whole universe getting incredibly messy.

As I set my tray down on the table, Jeremy wastes no time getting the conversation started. He leans in to Henry, who's seated across from him, and says, "Be prepared, Kimball. Panos is going to be hanging out with artsy types in the city and maybe he'll finally get laid." Jeremy looks back at me. "Just be careful or you may be getting sexed up by the Mr. Qs of the world."

Tommy Goliski walks up at that exact moment and says, "What's this?" He's accompanied by his usual underlings as well as Ali.

Ali smirks at Henry. "Hi, Henry."

"Hi, Ali."

"Hey, Evan. So how *is* your sex life?" Tommy wraps his arm around Ali's waist. I struggle to keep my composure. "I'm wondering, does Mr. Q like it on top?"

Henry chimes in. Jaw clenched. "Let's leave."

"We're not having a conversation. As in you and me." Tommy leans in toward Henry. "I'm talking to your boyfriend, who is apparently into older men." The underlings giggle. Literally.

I try to lighten the mood. "Hey, Tommy. Jeremy's a moron.

We can all agree on that." I look at Jeremy. "Right?" He nods.

"No. I'm actually curious. Is there a teacher-student scandal going on?"

"Probably in my parents' bathroom." Ali thinks she's being clever.

Henry's jaw continues to tighten. "Ali, don't."

Tommy shoves Henry's shoulder. "Don't tell her what to do. Just because you're not a real man doesn't make it okay to talk to a girl like that." Henry looks up and across the table at me. I covertly shake my head.

"Evan. Answer my question," Tommy demands.

I'm still looking at Henry. "No."

"No, you won't answer, or no, you haven't been laid?"

"The latter."

"What the fuck are you talking about? 'The latter.' Of course you haven't been laid when you talk like that."

"Something going on here?" Mrs. Lynwood appears out of nowhere. Now everyone's staring at us. "Everybody should find a seat and enjoy the pizza." Tommy and his band of zombies shuffle along. I exhale.

"That was close." Jeremy shoves practically a whole slice of pizza into his mouth.

"So what was Jeremy talking about?" Henry seems to be slowly calming down.

"His internship. Dude, where have you been? Mr. Q is all over it, and probably . . ." Jeremy's spitting out pizza as he talks.

Henry wipes his face with a napkin. "Hey, you're spraying me over here."

"Sorry."

I stare right at Jeremy. "Enough with the Mr. Q shit. Okay? It's not like that. Why are you always such a grade-A fuck? You wonder why Tess was never interested? Really? You wonder?" I get up. "I have to get to class."

"I'll walk you." Henry gets up too and we leave Jeremy alone at the table. Between Tommy's aggression and Jeremy's full-on stupid, I'm seething. I don't look back to see what he's doing and honestly, I don't care.

twenty-eight

The days leading up to Thanksgiving are some of the busiest at the deli, and next week will be even worse. I work every day, which is good news for a few reasons:

1. I can use the money.
2. I get very little attention at home as long as I'm working.
3. I have zero time for a social life.

The few moments of free time I do have are spent at the monastery.

Being surrounded by the statues gives me the illusion of not being alone, while not having to deal with actual conversations. Plus—no surprises. And it's still nice enough out to ride my bike. Going past Henry's neighborhood on the way is also an added bonus. I've tried to avoid major contact since the lunch-room incident. He understands. Right now, neither of us can risk too much drama. But my mind plays tricks and I think I see and hear him everywhere I go. I can definitely still smell him, and that makes me miss Henry even more. I pull out my journal and start to sketch him. I sketch Henry the way he looked when we were in his room. When we kissed. How his eyes looked at me as if they needed to see me in order to continue to shine.

I ride down Henry's street on my way back home. This is my fourth time riding past. I'm hoping he'll appear but at the same time I'm hoping he won't.

When he shows up, I stop, blinking my eyes, trying to make sure it's really him. I turn my bike around and ride back toward his house. We meet at the curb. I'm out of breath. He's wide-dimpled smiling.

"What are you doing?"

"Stalking."

"You can come in, you know. Claire's home. My parents are . . ."

"Have to get back home before it gets too late."

"Want to go for a drive tomorrow?"

"I have a family party to go to at my uncle's. You know. Every year."

Henry has both hands deep in his front pockets and he mumbles his words. "I think I'm going to go away for a few days. To one of those places. On our list."

"What?" I'm trying to make eye contact. Does he need to get away—from me?

"I just need a little break."

"Right." I'm not convinced.

We're both silent.

"You're doing your avoiding thing again." I don't say anything. "And I get it. I'm starting to figure you out. Push. Pull." He messes my already windblown hair. "It's only taken me years. Claire's going to go with me. I didn't want to go alone. I want to figure some stuff out."

"Okay. Um."

"What?"

I blurt out, "I want to go with you. So bad."

"Ev, I want you to. I didn't ask 'cause I know the situation at home."

"I hate being left out." I laugh uncomfortably at myself. "You know I'm not avoiding us 'cause I want to."

"I get. Like I said, I'm figuring you out." He smiles.

"Where are you going?"

"To see the albino squirrels of Olney, Illinois. It's about three hours away."

I chuckle. "Well, that sounds pretty perfect. I think I wrote that one down."

He nods. "I'll take pictures."

"And your parents are okay with this?"

"They said they were. It helps that Claire's coming."

"Right. She is their favorite." I smile.

"Asshole." He gently bumps his right shoulder into me.

"I'm glad you're going."

"You have the monastery, your drawings. I need something."

His voice drifts off. "Maybe now more than ever."

I look right at him and say, "What's it like? Being out to your family?"

"Some days it's like nothing. Everyone's just the same. Grumpy, loud, happy, stupid. You know. Other days, it's a thing."

"Bad thing?"

With a low voice and his eyes avoiding mine he says, "No. Just . . . I just want it to be like before. I don't want to be the *gay* son. The one everybody is trying so hard with. You know?"

I want to hug him right now and make him feel okay, but instead I say, "I don't. I mean, I think I do, but you know."

"Yeah. How is it? How has she been?" I can hear the nervousness in his voice.

"Okay. No major incidents. I'm keeping a low profile. Following the rules. Being a . . ."

"A good little soldier?" His eyes are dark. "You know I want to go over there, right? Go over there and talk to her. Tell her never to touch you again. Actually, I don't think I'd talk that much."

A part of me feels warm, in a good way, at what Henry is saying. No one has ever stood up for me like that. "You can never get involved. Henry? Look at me."

He stares at the sky, the ground. Finally, he looks at me. His eyes are wet. "I think about you in that apartment, and I get so fucking mad."

"You are not getting involved."

"I already am. I want to make it stop."

"I can take care of myself." He sighs. Finally, he leans his head in and touches his forehead to mine. We're outside. At the curb. In front of his house, and I don't flinch.

twenty-nine

It's the Sunday before Thanksiving. I pull my bike into the parking lot at my uncle's restaurant and look for a spot to lock it up. The place is packed. This may be the biggest turnout yet. I recognize some of the cars, but there's a bunch I don't. I look into the restaurant. I can almost make people out. It seems like everyone from my life, with the exception of my school friends, is here. The sooner I get in there, the sooner I can check this day off the list.

I enter and instantly my mother spots me. She's wearing a dark-blue fitted skirt and a cable-knit sweater with a silver cross necklace over it. The necklace is modest and tasteful, which is how my mother likes to appear. Her hair is down and beautifully blown out. She has her trademark nude lipstick on and a hint of blush. She's smiling and comes toward me with open arms. Is this for show or is it real? I can never tell. She hugs me and kisses my cheek. "Honey, you look so handsome," she says out loud. Like really out loud. She then turns closer to me, still smiling, and whispers, "You look like a prostitute in those pants."

She goes back to being the perfect host, escorting me around the restaurant by the arm. We walk up to a couple who have their backs to us. The man has a full head of dark hair and the woman is wearing a leather vest over a white sweater. She has leather knee-high boots that match the vest, and her hair is up.

"Helen and Dean, this is my beautiful boy I was telling you so much about," my mother lilts and, with elaborate hand motions, presents me. Like, *ta-da!*

Helen and Dean both turn around. They're smiling.

Helen exclaims, "Your son is even more handsome than you described, a true Greek man. Isn't that right, Dean?" She turns to her husband before finishing with, "How do you not have a girlfriend?"

"Ooooooh, we can fix that!" My mom is laughing. "Helen and Dean are new to town and to our church, but old friends of your uncle's. We saw them at church for the first time today. What a wonderful family they are! Greeks who praise the Lord and they have three beautiful children, also for the Lord."

Let me guess. One of these children is a girl around my age, and the poor thing has, unbeknownst to her, been chosen to be my wife.

"Dean is a successful doctor from Chicago and Helen a beautician. She used to have her own salon in the city and she's looking to open one here. Here in Kalakee! Isn't that wonderful? God has blessed them." My mother is giddy. It is a sight to behold when she is like this. She's looking around the room. "Helen, where is your beautiful daughter?"

Bingo.

"I'll go find her, Voula. You stay right here, young man." Helen straightens my hair like I'm her own.

"Dean, tell Evan about how you and your wife came to America from Greece with nothing. Nothing but your faith and hard work, and look at you both now! You are so blessed!" My mother turns to me, as if I have suddenly gone deaf. She loudly and slowly repeats herself and does her version of Greek sign language. *"They had nothing. Nothing. God and hard work blessed them."*

Just in time, here comes Helen with her daughter. "This is Maria." She presents her the way my mother presented me a few minutes ago. They might as well just have us sit on a giant lazy Susan when we're at this age, and spin us around at every Greek gathering. It would save so much "presenting time."

"Maria, this is Evan," Helen says.

My mother starts gushing like a fountain. "Oh, Maria, you beautiful girl. I just love your hair. Isn't she lovely, Evan?"

Maria smiles.

"Nice to meet you, Maria." I extend my hand, the perfect Greek gentleman.

"You too, Evan."

It's not that Maria isn't attractive. It's just the ridiculousness of this whole situation. Maria is dressed in what looks like a Halloween costume for a little girl, one who wants to be the princess of a pastel kingdom. It's so tight on top that parts of her exposed skin are purple around the areas where they meet the fabric. The bottom half sticks straight out and is layer upon layer of white, pink, green, and blue. I can't tell if she's picked this out herself or if this is Helen's doing.

It's amazing what my mother is able to forgive if you're Greek and the "right kind of Christian." If this was the same exact situation with someone from my school who was, say, a Lutheran, there would have been a nonstop fire-and-brimstone speech following this meeting.

"What grade are you in?" I try to make conversation.

"I start high school next year." Maria seems thrilled by this and I'm mortified. She's a child. Like, an actual child.

"Great. You must be so excited. Good for you."

"Evan graduates in the spring." My mother is now beaming at me with something resembling pride.

Helen seems impressed and proud too, which is completely weird. Clearly she's okay with presenting her maybe not even fourteen-year-old daughter to a guy who is going off to college. I continue to smile and say, "I just got here and I'd love to grab some food. So great to meet you all, and welcome to town."

I smile and start walking away. My mother follows me.

"What are you doing?" she whisper-yells.

"I'm sorry. I need to eat something."

I'm walking through the crowd looking for the food tables. I smile at everyone I pass. My mother is right beside me the whole time.

She's whispering in my ear. "You always think you're something special." She spots someone she knows, and waves and smiles. She calls out to them, "I'll talk to you in a minute, my dear. I must get the boy some food." She turns back to me. "She may be a little young, but you would wait for her. Who else would want you? You have to get yourself in while they are still impressionable and think you are better than you are." She waves at my uncle. "*So* beautiful, this party." Back to me. "In five years you could be married. Perfect time for you and for her. Don't be stupid. Also, don't be too proud of yourself because Helen complimented you. People compliment you because they feel sorry for how ugly you are."

Finally, I see the food. A long table brimming with everything a person could ever want and think of. Say what you will about this mess of a gathering, they know how to feed a crowd. I grab a plate and start at one end of the table.

"Mom, please just let me eat something. It's been a long day at work. It was unbelievably busy, plus I'm so tired."

"What are you tired from? You don't know tired." She picks up a plate as well. "You will eat something and then go back and socialize with that family and their daughter! Is that clear?"

I look at her and she's biting her lower lip with her teeth.

Hard. She used to do this all the time when I was younger and we were out in public. If I was doing, saying, or wearing something she didn't like, she would do this across the room and I knew it meant that once we got home, she'd beat me till I was cowering in a corner somewhere.

"There you are." My dad appears. He also grabs a plate. He leans in and kisses me on the cheek.

"Mom just introduced me to Helen, Dean, and their daughter Maria." I put six feta cheese–filled filo dough triangles onto my plate.

"Oh."

"You stay out of this, Eli! I'm thinking of our future. Someone around here has to." She takes her plate—with just a single piece of spanakopita—and storms off, smiling, of course.

My dad sighs. "How was work today?"

"So busy. It was crazy. There was never a moment when we didn't have at least ten people in the deli. They must be busing them in from other towns." I add a second story of food to my plate.

"It's the season. Don't forget to make the rounds and greet everyone. You can go home once you do, okay?" My father puts some melon on his plate and walks off. My mother swoops in, grabs my arm, and leads me in a specific direction. She's moving so fast that I drop my plate of food. She doesn't seem to notice. We're still charging forward.

"I'm glad you're done eating." *I didn't even start.* My

mother weaves us through the crowd. We settle near the booths by the corner of the restaurant that faces the parking lot. Seated in the booth are Helen, Dean, Maria, and two other kids.

"Here he is. He couldn't wait to get back to us. These are their other gorgeous children, Mani and Toula. Six and nine, right?"

Helen replies, "Yes. Good memory, Voula. Evan, what will you be going to college for?"

Here's my chance to really kill any hope these two Greek mothers have of ever blending our families. It's my passive-aggressive way of standing up for myself. "I'll be studying fine art."

"He hasn't decided yet, really." My mother bites her lower lip. "He really wants to be a businessman." She sits in the booth with them and motions me to join.

"Actually, I don't. I want to study fine art. And I'd love to join you, but it's getting really late and I have school tomorrow. There's homework." I know she can't outwardly argue this.

Helen is beaming right at me. "Such a dedicated young man."

My mother somehow finds her smile. "He really is. You know, he was at work all day today." She turns and fixes me with a level gaze. "Get home safely, dear."

thirty

It's Thanksgiving week, and walking to school the Monday before the holiday feels like a waste of time. It's really a do-nothing week. Everyone's so focused on being off for the holiday and the food. But maybe it's the crisp air, or the thought of the other day with Henry—whatever it is, today I'm feeling energized.

As I approach the entrance to the building, I notice everyone clumped together.

"Hey, Panos!" Jeremy breaks from one of the clusters and heads my way. "Where is Kimball? Dude, did you know about Henry? He really is a big gay boy, apparently." Jeremy says it loud enough for everyone to hear. I'm suddenly feeling queasy—nervous and scared for Henry. And for me.

Tommy Goliski chimes in from near the door, "He's not just a big dickhead, he wants one!" A bunch of laughter, because they're a bunch of easily amused idiots.

I look at Jeremy and he's snort-laughing. I'm disgusted. "Jeremy? What are you—"

"Panos, he's your friend. You guys spend soooo much time together. What's up? Huh? You know what's going on. You have to." He gives me a knowing look and then *winks*. He's reached a whole new level of douchery right now. One I may never forgive him for.

"They're probably butt buddies." Tommy smiles at me, and it's not a nice smile. "Is that why Henry's not in school today? His ass hurt too much?"

More laughter.

I say, "You guys are pathetic. You don't know anything about Henry." I sound calm, but my palms are sweating. And maybe the back of my neck. And my armpits. I start to walk toward the entrance—concentrating on one foot in front of the other—when Tommy grabs me by the backpack and spins me around.

"You know, I thought I could help you, but I can't fix a faggot." He continues spinning me as hard as he can.

Someone in the crowd yells, "Gay boys like it rough. Throw him to the ground!" I can't tell who says it because I'm whirling like a thrill ride at the Kalakee Harvest Carnival.

Suddenly I'm on the ground and Tommy and Scott Sullivan are kicking me, and Lonny Cho is trying to pull my pants off. I can see Jeremy just standing there. *Why the fuck isn't he trying to help?*

"They were probably doing it all this time," someone else yells, and then they're imitating Henry and me talking to each other.

"Do you want to play tennis this weekend?"

"Only if you bring the balls."

"Don't I always, big boy?"

Roars of laughter, and from what I can tell, more people are gathering around. Humiliating. My pants are around my knees—luckily my underwear is still on—and Tommy and Scott are now trying to flip me over on my stomach. I've worked so hard to protect myself, to not be exposed, to keep from making any waves at all. And now it feels like my whole world is crashing down around me.

"He's probably used to that position!"

Is that Jeremy? I can't tell anymore. My face is pressed to the concrete, and like that, I go flashing back. I hear the chanting of my mother and her church friends as they try to cast out the demons.

I am not evil.

I am not bad.

They are the bad ones.

The more Tommy and Scott try to push me into the ground, the angrier I get.

In a flash I see my mother holding me underwater, in the ocean. I can't breathe. Her hands are firm on my face as I jerk around. Suddenly, like images in a flip book, I see:

FLASH: My mother's firm grasp on my hair as she drags me from the living room into her bedroom.

FLASH: Her foot on my back, pushing me closer to the kitchen floor.

I grab hold of Tommy and Scott, and with strength and anger I didn't know I had, I push them off of me and onto the ground. I yank my pants up, leap to my feet, and then I unleash it all—all the anger, all the hurt, all the rage that has been building up inside me every time my mother has raised her hands against me. I let it all out.

And then I black out.

I open my eyes and I'm looking at ceiling tiles. White ceiling tiles with little pinholes in them. I scan the room and realize I'm in the principal's office on his sofa. I try to move but my chest hurts.

Why does my chest hurt?

Right, I was kicked there a lot.

Suddenly I can feel the throbbing in my jaw, nose, head, hands, and legs. I close my eyes and try to will myself to black out again and wake up somewhere else with different surroundings and circumstances. Maybe a different life. The door swings open into the room and I slowly open my eyes again.

"Mr. Panos, you're awake." Principal Balderini pulls up a chair and sits next to me. "How are you feeling?"

"Um." I try to sit up and immediately feel dizzy.

"Evan, please just lie down. The nurse cleaned you up and everything has been bandaged. She doesn't think you broke anything."

"Okay." I just lie there looking at the ceiling and wondering, How the hell do I explain this?

"Do you want to tell me what happened?"

"I was attacked."

"The others said you attacked them as well."

The more I open my mouth to speak, the more I realize how much it hurts to move it.

"How many stories are there?"

"Well, Scott and Tommy have their version and then there are a few opposing ones from the crowd."

"I was trying to protect myself."

"Protect yourself from what? Why did they attack you?"

I lie, "I don't know."

"We're going to investigate this. Apparently there's some cell phone video as well."

I mutter under my breath. "Great."

"I'm sorry?"

"I don't feel great. It hurts to move my lips."

"Luckily, as I said earlier, you haven't broken anything as far as we can tell. Your parents are outside and ready to take you to the doctor for X-rays and home. We'll get to the bottom of this. We do not tolerate any kind of violence in this school. But for the moment, I just want you to be well. Is there anything you want to tell me?"

"I'm sorry, sir."

"Just so you know, there could be some long-term suspension that you and your friends may be facing."

"Suspension?" I slowly get up and am now sitting on the sofa.

"We'll talk about that later."

I look away from the principal. I don't say anything. I've learned that after every beating I should become as silent and as small as possible.

"Evan?"

I'm still looking away as I say, "I didn't start this. I was attacked."

I look at him now. He's studying me.

"Who? Who started it? Tell me."

I don't say anything.

"We're going to investigate and find out what happened here. At the very least there will be a suspension. Across the board. It's a holiday week and right now you and the rest of those involved will be suspended from school until the Monday after Thanksgiving. I'm going to review everything that happened and we will all reconvene next week." His voice is firm yet calm.

I shake my head slightly and softly say, "Not fair."

"Now would be a good time for you to open up."

"It's difficult."

"Evan, you're a good kid. You never get into trouble. You maintain a very level presence. Don't let this one-time mistake define you. Just tell me what happened."

"I don't know. I blacked out."

He's silent for a moment. Then: "Maybe the video holds some answers. Okay? You may still have to speak to the police about this. Fighting on school grounds is a serious offense. I'll keep you and your family informed."

"Okay."

Mr. Balderini gets up and puts the chair back, then extends a hand in my direction. "Here, let me help you up."

I grab his hand and lift myself up. I notice for the first time that my knuckles are raw and my hands are all scratched up. I'm standing next to the sofa. "Thank you."

"Evan, if there's anything else, anything you remember, please call me."

My parents are right outside the office. They both take one look at me and their eyes widen. I haven't seen what I look like yet, but I'm figuring this would have worked better about a month ago for Halloween. I know my mom is going to be very upset that I won't look my best for Thanksgiving.

"Evan, let's get you home. You have an appointment with a doctor tomorrow." My father extends his hand.

"I can walk. Not too fast, but I can walk." I try to smile a bit to show that I'm okay. My mother looks horrified.

We get to the car, and once the doors close she bursts into tears. "What happened, my beautiful boy?"

I'm stunned.

"Evan, are you okay? What happened?" My father is looking at me from the rearview mirror.

"Where's my backpack?"

My dad says, "It's in the trunk."

"Who gave it to you?"

"The principal. We have it."

I feel around in my pockets and my phone is still in there.

"I bet String Bean is involved in this somehow. You cannot hang out with that boy again, do you hear me?"

"Vee, how could he? He's his best—"

"Don't be stupid."

I stay silent.

"They've ruined Thanksgiving. These boys. Ruined it. How are we going to take you anywhere looking like this? How are you going to be able to go back to work? You can't work looking like you do!"

Here's the deal about never being authentically loved by your parents: The most fucked-up gesture or morsel of compassion is like a warm blanket.

The rest of the ride is in silence.

• • •

In my room, I unzip my backpack. I let out as big a sigh as I can and quickly realize that it hurts to exhale or inhale, unless I do small, short breaths.

The journal is still there.

I can hear my parents arguing in the living room. Usually when they fight, I get as close to my door as possible and listen to see if she's mad at him. It's oddly comforting to hear them fighting about something other than me. This time, I know it's about me. I don't listen. I walk over to my closet, open one of the doors, and look at myself in the full-length mirror. Not as bad as I thought. I've looked worse. I have a bandage on my nose with a little dried blood coming out of my nostrils. My eyes are black. My jaw looks a little bruised and swollen, my lips are a bit beaten up, and I must have a cut over my left eye, because there's a bandage there.

My phone is vibrating. I take it out and look at the screen. It's Henry. I don't pick up. I take out my journal from my backpack and begin to draw. I draw my face. Not as it is right now, but without any cuts, bruises, or scars. It's clean, strong, and calm.

I can't hear my parents anymore. I wait. I listen. It sounds like they've stopped fighting. Shit, that means I'm going to have company. I quickly shove the phone back into my pocket. My door swings opens and they both come in.

"We've been invited to Helen and Dean Boutouris's house." My mother says this as if they have received a White House invitation and like we all don't already know it. Repeating good news is a thing.

The thing about Thanksgiving in our family is that as much as everyone loves food, Thanksgiving is one of those holidays when they wing it at the last minute. No planning, no traditional Thanksgiving feast, just a wait-and-see-what-happens attitude. And if we don't get invited somewhere, we've been known to drive the streets of Illinois on Thanksgiving Day looking for an open restaurant.

This is the same family that literally cannot let a Wednesday go by without an all-day menu planning and cook fest, no matter how much they have to work. They will shop, cook, and feast—as long as it isn't Thanksgiving!

I've wanted a traditional sit-down Thanksgiving meal for as long as I can remember, just not with my family.

"I'm so tired and I feel really . . ."

"Would you rather stay home?" Mom strokes my hair and rests the palm of her hand on my left cheek. She turns to look at my dad. "It may be best for him to rest." He looks at me, nods his head, and sighs. She turns her attention back to me. "I'll make you your favorite, pastitsio, okay?"

My pocket is vibrating again.

I try to casually place my hand over it and speak louder in order to muffle the sound. "Mom, you don't have to. I know how busy—"

"Don't be silly. I want to. Look at you. You should rest and eat." She goes over to my bed and turns down the covers. She pats the pillow. "Here. Get in bed. You need your rest. I will get all the food ready for you for the big meal. All you'll have to do is heat it up."

My dad clears his throat. "You should probably get some rest. Your mother and I are going to go to the grocery store to shop for the week. Rest. Please."

My mother says, "You have an appointment at Dean's medical office tomorrow at twelve fifteen."

"What?"

"Dean's a doctor and our friend now. We called Helen when this happened—"

My dad interrupts her. "*You* called Helen, not we."

"I made an appointment for you at his office. He'll see you tomorrow to make sure that everything is okay. I'll be cooking and your father will be at work. You'll have to take the bus. I'm sorry." She points to the bed again. I remove my shoes and get in. Fully clothed. "Oh, and we didn't tell them what happened. We said you were in a car accident."

"I'm sorry, what?"

"Tell him you were in someone else's car and it was a hit and run. We don't want them thinking that this horrible thing happened to you." She bends over and tucks me in. "We want to protect you."

She smiles and kisses my right cheek.

They both exit my room.

This kind of behavior always messes with my head. It makes me believe this can be real. That care, concern, and love are real. I long for this. I can see it right before my eyes. It's the normal that I want, but it's not real. *The question is: Can it ever be?* It makes me wish my mother would always be cruel and horrible and unforgiving, because at least that's something I can count on.

I wait to hear their car drive off.

Once they're safely gone, I look at my phone.

No messages, but there are a bunch of texts from Henry:

Call me!

R u ok?

Plz call me.

Claire & I r driving bck. Plz call.

Driving as fast as we can. B in twn soon!

And a text from Jeremy:

Hey Panos. U ok?

Fuck Jeremy. I ignore his text.

Instead I text Henry:

I'm home--all good--don't wrry--plz drive safe!

Henry instantly replies:

Bout 1 hr away--coming over.

Oh no.

No.

This is not a good idea.

No! U can't--plz. 2much crzy here right now.

Hopefully that will stop him.

But no.

Cming over. Have2!

You're just going to have to tell him.

I'm not allowed 2cu--it'll b 2much trbl frm parents.

Please, please let this be the thing that stops him. I can't deal right now and I need to deal. I need life to just be calm again, to go back to having everything in neat little compartments.

But what if I don't want to? What if that's not who I am anymore?

I feel this weird panic.

A few minutes go by, and no response from Henry. That's a good sign, but I probably upset him. Maybe if I call him, I can tell him exactly what I mean.

Just as I'm about to, another text comes in:

I'll park away frm apt. They won't c my car--u sneak me in-- will let u know when there.

thirty-one

Even though I haven't been able to sleep, my phone buzzing startles me out of a daze and I fumble for it.

I'm here.

Hey

Evan?

I start to type, but I'm groggy:

OK.

I get up and weave a bit getting to my bedroom door. I steady myself and head toward the front door. I look through the peephole and see him standing there. Even with the way a peephole can alter your features, he still looks like the guy I want to kiss more than anything else. I open the door. He looks at me and starts to cry.

"Do I look that bad?"

He leans in and places his head against mine. He pulls back

a little and whispers, "Are they here?" I shake my head. "I don't know where I can touch you. I don't want to make anything hurt."

"You couldn't possibly do any more damage. I never thought I'd say this, but we have to go into my bedroom." I'm leading him to my room. "My parents are at the store. I don't know when they'll be home, but I'm not supposed to see you. This is . . ."

"I'm so sorry. Ev, I'm sorry." He follows me to my room.

We enter and I close the door behind us.

"You didn't do this." I sit on my bed and look back at him.

"I did. I came out to my parents and somehow word must have reached school. This happened to you because you're friends with me. I shouldn't have said anything. I was being—"

"You didn't do this."

Henry stops and looks around my room. "I feel like I know this place, but I've never been in here. Everything is so . . ."

"It helps me. It helps to have everything in its place and neat."

He comes over and kneels in front of me. He puts his hands gently on my knees.

"I want to make every one of them feel pain. Who was it?"

"It doesn't matter. Really. I want things to calm down. Can they just be normal again, please?"

Right now. Here in my room with this boy, I feel wounded

and brave all at the same time. This boy—just looking into his eyes—makes me strong and vulnerable.

He lifts up from his knees slightly and we kiss. His hands are on the back of my head and mine are on his shoulders. He kisses my eyes. He moves to the cut above my left one and kisses there, too. Then to the bandage on my nose and then to my swollen and bruised chin. The last thing he kisses are my hands.

My parents are still out shopping. I'm taking a huge risk, but I want to. I turn off my phone. Henry lies next to me and we drift off to sleep quickly.

I'm suddenly awake and reach over to my nightstand. I turn on my phone. It's 3:19 a.m. And then I see the phone is filled with texts. I ignore them. Henry is curled up in a ball behind me. His head is wedged into the middle of my back and his left hand is wrapped around my waist. I try to slowly move my body away from his and out of bed. Everything feels extra achy and stiff. I shuffle toward the door and put my left ear to it. I do my usual checks to make sure the coast is clear.

"Ev?"

I go back to the bed as quickly and silently as possible. I lean in and whisper, "Shhh. We have to get you out before my dad wakes up. He's usually up by four."

Henry makes a face and whispers, "Why can't it be like this all the time? Minus you in pain and without us being in your parents' place. Other than that, like this all the time."

Right now, in this moment, he looks like he did all those times we'd go camping with his parents in Wisconsin. We'd wake up in the morning, early, just before the sun. His hair would be sticking up in the back like a crown, but all it took was a quick finger comb and it was back to normal.

His squinty eyes seem even more downturned at the edges, and his lips are so pink. I look at him and think the exact same thing, *Why can't it be like this all the time?*

"I'm going to go out and see if anyone's up. Get your stuff and be ready to go once I come back." I make my way to the door.

I unlock it and go out into the hallway. I take a few steps and peek into the living room. All clear there. There's a bathroom between my room and my parents'. I listen at their door. I hold my breath. I can hear snoring. My dad is definitely asleep. It's fifty-fifty with my mother. I walk back toward the door of my bedroom, stick my head into the room, and signal for Henry to come out.

The walk to the front door seems like the longest journey. Once there, I unlock it oh-so-quietly and turn to Henry. I give him a half smile and then look back down the hallway. He turns my head toward his and kisses me a little longer than I'm comfortable with in this situation. I push down on the door to open it, since I can minimize the squeaking by doing that. It still creaks and cracks a bit. He runs out and I close and lock it. I exhale. Was I holding my breath the whole time?

Walking back to my room, I hear my parents' bedroom door open. My mother pokes her head out and spots me.

"You finally up?" She starts to come out into the hall. She's tying her robe around her waist and walks past me. Once she's in the kitchen, I hear her ask, "You want coffee?"

"Okay." I walk into the dining area, which is open to the small kitchen.

Her back is to me. She's at the sink filling the coffeepot with water. She then fills the coffee maker and turns it on. She comes and sits opposite me at the table.

"I heard the door. Were you outside?"

I think quickly. "The cold air feels good on my face. The swelling and all."

She gets up, goes to the freezer, and grabs a bag of peas. She hands it to me.

"Here, put this on your face." She sits back down. "Your father didn't want to wake you last night. We got home after ten, went to the mall too. Did you eat anything?"

I shake my head. "I was tired. I just slept." I can hear the coffee start to brew.

"How are you feeling?"

"Okay."

We sit and look at each other. The six-year-old in me can't help but think, *Maybe this is a new her, a new us. Maybe from*

*now on she will change, be like other mothers are. Maybe
everything will be okay.*

"Your life isn't hard." She looks right into my eyes. "You
have a roof over your head. You have both your parents. You
have food. And that man in there"—she points in the direction
of their bedroom—"he sacrifices everything for us."

"I know. He does."

"But you're ungrateful."

Something turns in my stomach. I'm thinking, *No, no.
Don't do this. Don't be this person. Don't be you.*

She sounds calm. There's no yelling or exaggerated hand
gestures, which somehow makes it worse. She gets up to grab
three mugs and the sugar from the cupboard above the sink and
the cream from the fridge. She puts them down on the table in
front of me and sits back in her chair.

"What are you going to do for him?"

I'm so lost in my thoughts that it takes me a minute. "Who?"

*Don't say anything else, because if you do it will only be
worse. Don't say a word.*

She says, "Your father. We can't pay for you to go to college. You don't want to help him open the restaurant? You
would work for a stranger and not for your own father? That's
not why we came to this country. Are you not proud of your
family?"

She looks down and shakes her head. With her head still

down, looking at the dining table, she begins to wipe dust off the surface—where there is no dust—with the left sleeve of her robe.

"Then you go ahead and get into this." She looks up, still wiping her sleeve on the table, and runs her eyes over all my battle wounds. "I used to look like that."

This last line is said very faintly and far away. I want to ask her to repeat it, but she gets up and grabs the coffeepot from the kitchen. It's filled with light-brown liquid. Her coffee is always really weak, and then she adds so much cream that you can't even make it out as coffee anymore. This is one of the things I know about my mother.

She grabs a small dessert plate from the cabinet above the sink to the left. With one hand she places the plate on the table and the coffeepot on top of it, neatly, precisely. She sits back down.

"My brothers used to beat me till both my eyes were swollen shut and my lips were so cut I couldn't eat." She pours what looks like a full cup of cream into her mug, then adds a splash of coffee. I'm still. My father would say I didn't know what she'd been through. That her life wasn't easy. I just never knew the details. I never cared to ask. Am I a horrible son?

"Because they didn't want me to disgrace the family. They raised me. No parents. They did. I had big ideas. Like you. Big ideas for myself. I wanted to be a singer." She smiles a little at the memory. "But that was considered work for loose women." Her voice goes flat. "Small village. Small minds. I would sneak off when they were at work to take lessons with a woman in the next town over." She adds two teaspoons of sugar to her coffee. "They found out. They beat me to teach me about honor. About a woman's place."

She looks at me and I look at her. Neither one of us says anything. The words are there between us, and I want to say something but I don't know what. I'm trying to see my mother as a girl, as someone who would sneak off and try to live her dreams.

Finally, she says, "You've disgraced us, don't you see? Everyone looks at us, everyone at the church, here in our neighborhood. We live in a small village. They all talk. You don't think they know what you are? You don't think I know what you are?"

I am going cold everywhere, inside and out.

"You make our life so much harder. My beatings taught me lessons. You. You learn nothing." She takes another sip of her coffee. And then she says to me, her only child, "They should have killed you."

From someplace very far away, I hear the bedroom door open and my dad clearing his throat. Every morning the throat clearing is intense. Maybe it's all the years of smoking, or maybe that's what happens when you're old. He's headed to the bathroom, where a good solid five minutes of hacking, coughing, and throat clearing will take place.

My mother leans in, looks right at me, and lowers her voice to a hush. "Die. If this is who you are."

And now blood has turned to ice. My limbs have turned to ice. I am frozen.

She leans back in her chair. She takes me in. Scans my face with all its evidence of violence. Her eyes squint. The corners of her mouth turn upward slightly.

My dad enters the dining room. "Morning."

She turns to him and smiles. "Morning, my love."

thirty-two

I'm sitting in the waiting room of the Kalakee Medical Offices.
It looks like I'm the only person in here under eighty years old.
There's a man and a woman directly across from me and he is
leaning slightly on her.

There's a woman sitting by herself to my left with a cast on
her right foot, below the knee. On my right there are two men,
probably slightly younger than the couple, and they are both
asleep. Or dead. I can't tell.

I feel dead inside.

"Evan Panos?"

I raise my hand. Everyone, except the sleeping/dead men,
looks in my direction.

"Use that door and come on back, honey." The nurse smiles
and points to a door next to the reception window. She leads me
to a small room and has me take a seat on the examining table.

"So, I hear you were in a car accident?" She inspects my face.

"Yes."

"Were you driving?" Her hands are on either side of my neck, feeling around.

"I wasn't. Um, I was . . ."

"Have any trouble focusing?"

All the time.

"No. I feel fine."

"Where does it hurt?" She places her hands softly yet firmly on either side of my chest.

"It hurts a little there and my hands." She takes my hands in hers and examines them. "How did your hands get so beaten up?"

I just look at my hands. How did they get so beaten up in a "car accident"? I try to come up with an answer quickly but my mind is not cooperating.

"Were you wearing your seat belt? Were you flung into the windshield or door?"

"Yes. The windshield."

"So no seat belt?"

"No, I was wearing a seat belt. Always. Just the force of the impact and my hands just . . ." My voice drifts off.

She picks up her chart, looks down at it, and starts to write. "Well, you may have just slammed them into the dashboard or something. No bones look broken, but we'll X-ray everything."

"Yes." I am nodding. "The dashboard."

"Take off your shirt, please." I don't move. "Evan?"

"It's not—"

"It's okay. I do this all the time. It's my job. Shirt, please." She points to my shirt. I start to take it off. "What's all this?" She comes closer and starts looking at my chest, the sides of my body, and then she goes around and examines my back. She comes around and looks right at me. "The doctor will be with you in a minute or two." She exits.

I sit on this thin piece of paper that's covering the examining table and think of what the hell I'm going to say to Dr. Boutouris. My life in this town, when I step back and look at it as an observer, is not one worth fighting for. Is it? I don't want this life, so why do I keep fighting for it?

I don't know how long I sit here before the door opens and Dr. Boutouris enters.

He stands in front of me. He seems taller than the last time I saw him, at my uncle's restaurant, but I wasn't sitting at the time.

"Hey there, Evan. Sorry to hear about your car accident and I'm sorry you won't be joining us for Thanksgiving."

I am avoiding eye contact. My entire body has gone rigid. Please don't ask about all the scars.

He starts to put his hands on either side of my chest to feel my ribs. "The nurse already checked there," I say more loudly than I intended.

This catches him off guard and he steps back. He then moves closer in and starts examining all the bruises, cuts, and wounds. He is very careful, as if I might break. He doesn't know I'm already broken.

"Have you gotten into any other kinds of accidents?"

I just blink at him.

"Evan?"

"I'm here for X-rays. That's what my—"

"Son, your entire body is covered. This isn't all from a car accident. It can't be."

"I fall off my bike sometimes . . . also, I'm not very coordinated in general."

He doesn't say anything, and I wonder if he believes me. I wonder if he sees other kids like me.

"I don't even feel it anymore when I fall." I try to laugh it off.

He frowns at me. "Do your parents know about all these—"

"Do they know how klutzy I am? Oh yeah. I've always been this way." More nervous laughter. "I'm sorry I won't be able to make Thanksgiving, though."

He's still frowning. "I'll get the nurse back in and she'll take you to the X-ray room."

• • •

An hour later, I'm standing outside the medical office. I text Henry:

Done.

He texts back almost immediately.

B right there.

"Get in." He swings the door open from inside the car.

I get in. I take a breath for the first time since I walked into the doctor's office.

"Where to?"

"I need to get back home."

He pulls out of the parking lot and then glances over at me. "So. What did—"

"They took X-rays. He asked about all the other bruises."

"Did you say anything?" I just look at him. "Right."

"I don't know if he believed me."

"Do you ever—do you ever think of talking to anyone? Like him or the principal? I don't know, someone other than me?"

It's not like I haven't thought about it. "It's hard enough at home."

We drive for a few blocks in silence. I can feel him thinking, feel him wanting to fix this. But he can't fix this or me.

I say, "Thanks for picking me up."

"Ev, have you checked any emails or texts other than mine?"

"Why? Jeremy keeps texting me but I don't want to read

them. I don't want to deal with him right now—or maybe ever."

"You may want to look at them."

Something in his voice makes me pull the phone out of my pocket and scroll through Jeremy's texts.

Henry's voice is a little shaky. "Is there a video text?"

"Uh. Yeah, actually. I see one." I hit Play. Henry is silent.

The more I watch, the warmer my face gets. My face must be the color of a pomegranate.

Oh.

Shit.

Henry pulls the car over. "Are you okay?"

I set the phone down. I stare straight ahead. My lips and tongue feel numb. I'm so embarrassed. My hands are resting on my lap but I can't feel them. I know they're there, but they feel like nothing. "Ev?" I keep staring out the windshield. The sky is so clear. Unseasonably so. This time of year the sky is usually gray with lots of clouds, the big, puffy kind.

"I don't remember any of this." Which makes this whole experience even more mortifying. My gaze hasn't changed and the feeling in my hands hasn't returned.

"You don't have to—"

"It's probably online by now. My parents will eventually hear about this. Or see it." I think I can start to feel my left hand. "You know, I've been so worried that all my worlds would collide. Everything that I've worked so hard to file in the appropriate place would somehow escape." I stop staring out the window and turn to look at Henry.

"It's funny, but I never thought that this was something I had to worry about. That *I* was the one to worry about. All this time, I thought it was my mom or Gaige or the pastor or everyone else. But it turns out, it's me."

thirty-three

I write:

Where ru right now?

Jeremy texts back:

Just getting out

Can u come to the apartment?

B right there

Clearly I'm full of some kind of abnormal confidence to invite Jeremy—anyone, really—over to where we live. Even when my parents are out, I usually don't have the courage.

"Damn, Panos."

"Come in."

"Seriously? *Come in?* What happened to *don't ever set foot in my house?*" He walks past me, and now he's standing on our floor, on my mother's floor. "I've never been inside these apartments before. Not bad."

"Do you want something to drink?" Even when I'm pissed I can't help myself.

"I'm good."

I say, "Sit."

Jeremy sits in the center of the sofa—my mother's sofa—and he looks completely out of place, like he's one more piece of me that doesn't belong here.

I don't sit. I stand. I say, "There's a better way to say this, but hell if I know what it is right now. What the fuck is your problem?"

"Panos . . ."

"No. You get so much . . . I let you get away with so much. The Mr. Q bullshit, Tess, everything. I keep believing that there's a better person in there."

His head is down.

"And yet you continue to find new and shitty ways to prove me wrong!" I'm pacing. "I didn't even know about what I did that day. I don't remember anything."

"You must have blacked out or some shit." He rubs his neck, still looking down. "I didn't know what to do, man. I was scared. I felt responsible and . . ."

"What? Wait. . . ."

"Mrs. Kimball spoke to my mom about Henry. She told her about him coming out. You know, my mom and her have been friends for—"

"And you told the whole school?"

"No, man. Dude, I told no one." He looks at me briefly and then puts his head back down.

"Jeremy, don't fuck with me right now. I've got nothing to lose, so don't—"

"It was my mom." He looks back up at me. "Not the school. I guess she called her friends and . . ."

"Real classy."

"I'm sorry, man. I was scared."

"Yeah. You said that."

"So, you saw the video."

I nod.

"What—"

"I don't know."

"Do your parents know anything?"

"Not yet. I don't think so. I mean, they know about the fight but not about this part."

"It's a good thing they don't get online, right? It helps to be Old World sometimes." He's trying to lighten the mood.

I just toss him a look. Probably one I've gotten from my mother, because he goes all stiff and straight. "It's only a matter of time before a 'friend' tries to *help* by telling them that a video exists where I come out as gay and tell everyone that I'm in love with Henry Kimball!"

"I want to make this better. And listen, I don't care what you and Kimball do. Really, man. I just want you to—"

"What? What else do you want me to do, Jeremy? Huh? What's wrong with me?"

"Panos . . ."

"No. Why do I let people treat me like this?" I'm back to pacing and now I'm shaking my head as I speak. "I allow it. I make excuses for it. It's okay that she beats me 'cause *her life was hard*." I stop and turn to face Jeremy. I bend down and get right in his face. "Even when I see the fuckery I *still* let more shit happen."

I can tell he's completely lost. I go back to pacing. "I let people treat me badly and when they actually don't, I run. I avoid. I fucking say *no* to something that can be good for me."

"Evan. What did you say? Who beats you?"

I stop and look at Jeremy. I was right to believe there's a better person in there. I can see that guy in there. Jeremy just hasn't met him yet.

thirty-four

It's Thanksgiving. And three days since the incident at school. So far, my parents have said nothing.

"Want to go for doughnuts?" my dad says, entering my room.

"It's late, for us."

"It's never too late for doughnuts." He looks at his watch. "It's just after nine."

"Are they open today?"

"Yes. Always."

"Okay." I grab my jacket and baseball cap and follow him down the hall.

"Vee, we're going." He yells this from the front door as he opens it.

She appears from the bedroom with a bunch of clothes draped over her arm. "Not too late. I want you both to help me decide what to wear for this afternoon."

"See you soon." He closes the door behind us as we exit.

Linda must have the day off. There's a new person working the counter.

"What can I get you two?" She's older than Linda. I think. Friendly but in a much more reserved way. She has dyed, bright-red hair and matching lipstick. Her nails are painted a turquoise color.

"Two coffees, a cruller, and two chocolate glazed." My dad orders without any hesitation.

I say, "I don't know if I should have two." For some reason I want to punish him, to make him feel bad.

"Take the other home for later. How are you feeling?"

"Great. Amazing."

He swallows, looks down. Looks back up with this dumb, hopeful look. "It's all healing. I can tell."

"Yeah."

"Your mother is putting all her hopes on this restaurant idea. She's really invested emotionally."

"You?"

The waitress appears. "Two chocolate glazed. Coffees and two crullers." She places everything in front of us.

"I only wanted one cruller."

"You can take the other home." She smiles and walks away.

My dad smiles and takes a sip of his coffee. "I want the restaurant, I do, and the fact that people are helping us, well, it's great."

"Nervous?"

He nods while eating. "One of the cooks at work has a daughter who goes to your school."

"Oh."

"She was there the day of the fight." He takes another bite and a swig of coffee.

"Oh." I place both my hands on either side of my coffee mug and stare into it, wishing it was a portal that I could drop into. A portal that would take me away to another world, far away from this one.

The waitress is back. "You guys need anything else? More coffee?"

"Yes, please." My dad lifts his mug to meet her coffeepot.

"You, dear?"

"No thank you."

She hesitates. She's studying me. *Don't do it. Don't ask what happened to me.*

"Do you mind if I—what happened, honey?" She examines my face.

"He stood up for himself." My dad smiles at her. It's a sad smile. I feel a tightness in my throat.

She smiles back, notices a couple of new customers at the other end of the counter, waves, and heads toward them.

I say, "Are you going to eat the second cruller?"

"You want it?"

"No. Just checking."

"I'm sorry about dinner tonight. It's probably best that you rest, right?"

"So you know about what happened?"

I see my mom's face. I hear her voice as she told me she wishes I were dead.

My dad nods and says, "She just wants things to be perfect, and right now she thinks . . ."

"I'm broken."

He stares at me. I wait for him to say something, to tell me I'm not broken, that she's broken, she's the one. But instead he leans back a little and reaches into the right front pocket of his jeans and pulls something out. He places it on the counter. "It's still on the lot, but it's been paid for. I got him down to seven hundred fifty dollars. Can you believe it?" He takes another sip of coffee.

I stare down at the keys. The key ring is a bright-yellow plastic band with *Dick's Used Cars & Trucks* stamped in the middle of it in black lettering on one side. The address and phone number for Dick's is on the other.

"He's obviously closed today, but he'll be open tomorrow. It's a big day for him, the day after Thanksgiving."

"Dad . . ." I don't really know what I'm about to say, but I feel I need to say something.

He's looking straight ahead. "You're going to need it."

"What does Mom—"

"She doesn't know yet. I'll take care of it. Pick it up when you want."

As we walk into the apartment my dad announces, "We brought doughnuts!" My dad places the box on the kitchen table.

From the bathroom, my mother's voice: "Be right out. Just drying my hair." She comes out still wrapped in a towel, her hair and makeup perfectly done. "Both of you come here." She's walking toward the living room. She has three skirts and three blouses each on a separate hanger and they are all draped over the back of our burgundy velvet wingback chair.

"Which outfit?" She pulls out the first option—a black-and-white-checked wool skirt with a modest slit on one side and a black V-neck blouse with long sleeves. She holds it up to her. "This one?"

The contradictions sometimes are crazy making. She constantly berates me for not being the "right kind of man" and yet she has wanted me to style her hair and pick outfits for her since I was five.

My dad examines it and sits down on the sofa before adding, "It's good. I like it. Classic."

"Or this one?"

The next outfit is a camel skirt, very boxy, almost sacklike with a white cable-knit sweater on top and a paisley scarf.

I make a face and say, "It's washed out."

"Don't be so quick to judge." She holds it back up again.

"Evan's right. That does not look good. Too blah."

She tosses that outfit aside and gathers her last choice. She holds it up. "This is your last option!" It's a navy asymmetrical skirt with white stitching on the pockets and around the waist. The blouse is a white, turquoise, and green geometric print with a high neck and a solid black horizontal three-inch band all around the bottom. This one is the most interesting and works best with her coloring.

"This is the one," I say, and head to the kitchen for a doughnut. I grab a chocolate glazed and walk back into the living room. "I'm going to bed. I'm tired. Have a good time."

My mother smiles at me. "Get rest. Don't forget to eat when you get up. There's a pastitsio in the freezer." And she turns to iron her blouse.

thirty-five

In the dream, I'm standing in the center of the statue room in the monastery except that only the statue leading the way is in there with me. He's closer to the window than he has ever been. His hands are outstretched and his fingertips are touching the glass. I look around and wonder how the rest of the statues were moved and where to. I walk closer to where the remaining statue is and look out in the direction he's facing. And there are the rest. They're outside, assembled across the lawn.

The Army is scattered all about. The others are just past the wall that surrounds the property. I move right beside the one inside. He's still looking out the window, but now he seems even closer to it. His hands look like they can break the glass. It feels warm and stuffy in the room. I smell smoke.

I turn around and the place is on fire. I can feel my body heating up, yet my legs are frozen.

The sound of glass breaking shakes me out of it. I turn to

look at the statue next to me. Both of his hands are outside the window. The Army is lined up against the outer wall and I can barely make out the others.

Boom!

Boom!

I'm startled awake by loud thumping. For a minute, I don't know where I am. I look toward my bedroom door. It's open. My parents must have opened it before they left. The thumping is getting louder. It's coming from the front door. It seems like I've been asleep for a week. I actually have to place one of my arms against the hallway wall to steady myself. *What the hell?*

I stand up as straight as I can and feel the soreness on the left side of my body. I must have received more blows on that side.

"I'm coming!"

I press myself up to the door and look through the peephole. I open it slowly. He's standing there holding two large, brown grocery bags and sporting half of his usual full dimply smile. His eyes are sad and sparkly at the same time. Inside I'm bursting with joy at the sight of him, but I awkwardly try to contain it.

"You have to let me in. It's a holiday tradition that if someone shows up to your house with turkey on Thanksgiving, you show them in or . . ."

Henry holds up the bags.

"Or what?" I say, half smiling back at him.

"Or they just come in anyway." He walks in past me, making his way into the kitchen.

I look outside, in all directions, just in case my parents are out there somewhere, before closing and locking the door.

"You can't be here." I'm trying to convince myself that I want him to leave, even though I don't. I want him here. With me.

He's unpacking all these containers. "And you cannot *not* have a traditional holiday meal. Plus my mom would destroy me if I didn't drop this off. She spent the past twenty-four hours making and packaging all this." He removes the last container, which looks like it's some sort of sauce. No, it's gravy. Mrs. Kimball packed gravy.

"Is that why you're here? Because she'd be . . ."

He turns around and puts his right hand firmly behind my neck. He's inches from my face. His eyes are wet and I can tell he's holding his breath.

"That's not why I'm here."

He kisses me, pulls me even closer, and I can feel him right up against me.

I wrap both my arms around him. We're in the kitchen and the thought that this is happening in my parents' house right now should make me nervous.

But it doesn't.

"I love you, too." He whispers the words.

I put my head down and onto his chest. He kisses the back of it.

I lift my head and look at him. I take short, quick gulps of air, trying to stop the tears from coming.

"It's okay." He is looking right at me, both his hands on the back of my head. "You can cry. I won't let anyone hurt you again."

As he finishes those words, the seal rips apart. Tears come streaming down my cheeks, and his hands move from the back of my head to either side of my face now. It's as if he's trying to catch them.

Is this what it feels like to be safe, to have someone care no matter what or who you are?

"I won't hurt you."

I take Henry's hand and lead him to my room.

thirty-six

We're both naked and under the covers. Henry is on his side, looking at me and smiling.

"That smile is a problem," I say.

He smiles bigger.

"Seriously. I'm going to need some sort of shield or barrier from it."

"You seemed immune to it for years. How is just now a problem?"

"That's just what I made you think."

He starts to tickle me, which he quickly realizes is not a good idea.

"Ow!"

"I'm sorry. I forgot."

"Some moves I can't do."

"Lucky for me the ones you can are very enjoyable."

"Fuck you."

"So, you went into avoiding mode the last couple of days."

"I was embarrassed."

"I've never had anyone fight for me like that or yell out that they love me. It was . . ."

"Embarrassing. Mortifying. Humiliating. I came out in a video *and* told the whole school I'm in love with you. My big moment and I have no memory of it."

"At least we have it on video."

"For the entire world to see."

"I have to say, you pummeling those guys was kind of a turn-on. Is that wrong?"

"Just don't expect it as a general rule. As you can see, I didn't exactly walk away unharmed."

He says, "Come here." I lean into his chest. "I don't want you doing anything like that again. I'm sorry. I wasn't trying to make light of it."

"It's all crazy. All of it."

This. Henry. Me. Henry and me. Here. In my bedroom.

"Any word from your parents?"

"I think my dad knows. He bought me a car."

"What?"

"That '94 Tercel. He said I'm going to need it."

"Does your mom . . ."

"She doesn't know about the car or school. Yet. Believe me, I'd know it if she did."

Henry takes a deep breath and widens his eyes.

I say, "We should probably eat and then you have to go. What time is it?" I reach over to my bedside table for my phone. "Just after six."

"They'll be out till at least ten, don't you think?"

"I think, but I'd rather be safe."

I get up and start to put my clothes back on.

"Do you have to do that?" Henry asks.

"What?"

"I just like the way you look."

For as long as I can remember, my mother has told me the opposite. She actually looks for specific negative physical details to point out. When I was little she'd run her right index finger down the bridge of my nose to the tip. She wanted to make sure I wasn't getting my father's *hook*, as she called it. I didn't need another disadvantage on *my already ugly face*.

I lift up my boxers. Henry gets up and walks over to me. He puts his hands on my waist and stands as close as possible.

"Your legs are gorgeous. I don't want to stop looking at you."

"Just my legs?" I tease.

"Everything, Evan Panos. Everything about you is gorgeous. I'm going to the bathroom. Meet you in the kitchen." He kisses me, slips on his boxers, and exits.

I open the doors to my closet and look at myself in the full-length mirror. I've never really looked at my body, I mean *really* looked at it. So much of my identity has been based on other people's views of my physicality that I've never really wanted to look.

Whenever I step out of the shower, I always put a towel around all of me as quickly as possible and avoid catching my image in the mirror. When I happen upon my reflection in a store window I'm always startled by the person I see. I skillfully avoid being in photographs and I never take any selfies.

But right now, standing here in front of my mirror, I force myself to take a long look. To see what Henry sees. I notice my chest, my arms, my waist, and then I lift my boxers to expose more of my legs. It's like discovering something for the first time.

Maybe I'm not so ugly after all. Maybe no one is really ugly, and maybe no one has the right to call someone that or tell them that they are. Maybe the only real ugliness is what lives inside some people.

I close the doors and head out to the kitchen.

Henry goes, "We even have a whole pumpkin pie."

"We're not going to eat a whole pie. You have to take the rest home."

"Mom wanted to send it over for you and your family. It's Thanksgiving and she thought—"

"My family wouldn't understand." I start setting the dining room table. Henry enters the dining room carrying plates of food and puts them in the center of the table. I go into the kitchen and take silverware out of the drawer.

As I set the table, I channel my mother. "Sit down—we should start. This looks incredible. I can smell the stuffing."

Henry loads his plate with turkey, green beans, mashed potatoes, stuffing, and gravy. I watch as his fork weaves past the cranberry jam that's in the middle of the table.

"Your mom is not going to be thrilled knowing you're not taking any of that."

He shoots me a look. "You and my dad are the only two people I have ever met who like that shit."

We eat in silence for a minute, and the food is good, like really good.

Finally I say, "They're okay with you not being with the family?"

"They wanted you at the house with us, but they knew you had to rest." He says this between mouthfuls of turkey and mashed potatoes. "Plus I was there all morning for the Kimball Thanksgiving breakfast and I'll be there tonight for another round of pie or something."

I pour gravy over my potatoes and take a bite. "This is the best meal I've ever had. Maybe the best anything I've ever had."

Henry raises his eyebrows. "Better than . . ."

"Almost."

"It's hard to tell—you're kinda making the same sound."

"Shut up, Kimball."

"Ugh, don't last-name me like that. That's a Jeremy thing."

"Sorry. Let's not talk about him right now. Actually, let's

just focus on what's happening here. This feels like . . . I don't know, it's . . . this meal is perfect. Please thank your mom for all this." I wave my fork over the whole table and then point it at Henry and make a circle around him. "Thank her for *all* of this!"

We both laugh.

"Tess would die right now," I say.

"What?"

"She has a major crush on you. You know that, right? She told me. She'd fucking die."

Henry shakes his head in disbelief and says, "So, am I not going to see you this weekend?"

"Not avoiding. Just don't know."

"Keep me posted?"

I nod. "I have to work. Weekend after Thanksgiving—going to be crazy at the deli. On Sunday, well, you know. *Sunday*." I help myself to another scoop of mashed potatoes. "How were the albino squirrels?"

"Claire said she saw one. I never saw them. *They* avoided me as well. Maybe it's me?"

"It's not you. No one—not even squirrels—would want to avoid you."

Henry half smiles.

I get to see half the dimples.

"I never wanted to avoid you."

He full smiles and says, "When are you going to pick up

your car? And what did you say to your dad?"

"I don't know, and not much."

Henry puts his fork down. "What are we going to do about Monday? About going back to school?"

I was hoping to avoid the subject, because I don't know what to do.

"Ev, everything has changed. The whole school knows we're gay. You're in this situation because of me and now we . . ."

I set my fork down. For some reason, right this moment, it's all clear. I hear myself say, "We just tell the truth."

Henry looks at me.

"We can't go back and all of a sudden pretend—"

"I don't feel comfortable dragging you into this," he says.

"I'm not going to pretend that this isn't happening. You saw the video. I don't want to go back to the way things were before."

I pick up my fork and stab some turkey. I focus on bouncing it in and out of my mashed potato mound until it's covered with them. I look up at Henry. "Everything has changed and I'm glad." *Maybe I've changed too.*

I put the giant mashed potato–wrapped turkey into my mouth and start chewing.

Henry is laughing. "You look ridiculous."

I chew with my mouth open so that Henry can see the mashed potato literally oozing out. I try to speak. "Ith thaa a pobum?"

"You're my problem. You're a real problem." Henry is looking at my ludicrous mashed potato–filled face as if he's simultaneously seeing the most amazing and gross thing ever.

He gets up and walks over to where I'm sitting and proceeds to kiss me, fake passionately, while mashed potatoes are flying out of my mouth.

"Stop it." I can't keep from laughing. The more I try to stop, the more potatoes and bits of turkey go flying. "I think I just snorted some potato. C'mon!"

He stops trying to make me laugh and takes a napkin and proceeds to wipe the rest of my face. We both catch our breath. Henry gets down on his knees in front of my chair and rests his head on my lap.

"Ev, I've wanted this for so long. I can wait a little longer if you need more time."

I run my fingers through his hair. "You think you're the only one who wanted this?"

And it hits me. *It's always been Henry.*
Always.

thirty-seven

It's a little after ten p.m. and they're not home yet.

I'm lying flat on my bed with one of my pillows half on my head and half off. I can still smell Henry's hair on it. After he left I looked at my face in the bathroom mirror for a really long time. The bathroom has the brightest, harshest light, and I wanted to make sure I saw everything. Had anything changed? Did I look any different? I couldn't tell.

I hear the sound of a key turning in the front door, of the front door being unlocked. I get up and stand in the middle of my room. I'm so nervous. *Why am I so nervous? Oh yeah, because I just had sex with a boy. Not just any boy—but with Henry Luther Kimball.*

The boy I love.

And the sky isn't cracking in half, and God isn't striking me down. And I am still standing here when I hear my mom's voice calling me.

I head out to the hallway and see them in the living room. They look like they're in an okay mood. This is a positive sign. My dad's on the sofa. He's kicked his shoes off and my mom isn't yelling at him to put them in the closet. Another good sign. Already we're off to an A-plus start. She's standing in front of the velvet wingback chair and removing her earrings. She spots me.

"Come here. We want to tell you all about our night. They all send their love, and Maria missed you. Remember Maria? She kept asking about you all night, didn't she, Elias?"

My dad nods his head. "Yes. She did."

My mom motions to the other wingback chair. "First, tell us about your night. What did you do? Sleep? There's so much food here." She points to three plastic bags on the coffee table. "They would *not* let us leave without practically giving us a whole other turkey and all the sides. Helen even baked an extra pie for us to bring home to you."

"Wow." I sit down.

"Do you want me to make you a plate? Did you make yourself anything?"

"I'll put it in the fridge for tomorrow. I'm good right now, unless you guys want a snack." I spring up and carry the bags into the kitchen. I'm worried about staying in front of my parents—especially my mother—for too long, just in case they notice something different about me.

"We are stuffed just like that turkey! I may have a Greek

coffee, though," my dad calls.

"Okay, I got it. Stay in the living room. Mom, do you need anything?"

"Just some water, sweetheart."

Fuck. This is not a good sign. *Sweetheart?*

I bring her the water. "Your coffee is on the stove, Dad. So, tell me about your night." I'm trying to deflect the questions about my evening away from me. I take a seat.

As my dad starts to describe the evening, my mother says, "Evan, are you not wearing underwear?" She is staring below my waist.

"Mom. Please. I'm wearing sweatpants."

"Voula, leave the boy." My dad stretches out on the sofa, yawning.

"You're not wearing underwear. I can tell, the way everything flops around. I hope you didn't go out like that and announce such things to the neighborhood."

I get up to check on the coffee.

My dad starts talking about the evening again. He's trying to distract her from me, to get her back on track.

My mother calls out, "You really did miss a beautiful evening. Beautiful. They have a gorgeous house, of course, because they have money and Helen is a wonderful housekeeper. She cooks, cleans, and knows how to be a lady. Dean, of course, is a doctor, as you know."

These, along with being a good, godly woman or man, and

being Greek, are extremely important qualities for someone to possess in order for my mom to even consider them as someone worth her time.

"Plus they are godly people. So you know their kids will grow up to be the right kind of adults."

Unlike me, who will be the wrong kind of adult.

I walk into the living room with my father's coffee and hand it to him.

He sits up straight on the sofa and adjusts his shirt. "Thank you."

"Sit, sit, we have so much more to chat about." My mother settles into her chair and looks up toward the ceiling, almost as if she's being nostalgic for something that took place years ago. "Dean is so handsome and a true gentleman. He's also very smart with business and had some great ideas for your father, didn't he, Elias?"

My dad nods, taking a sip of his coffee. "This is perfect, Evan." He adds, "Just the way I like it." He winks at me and takes another sip.

My mother continues. "They were very taken with you at your uncle's party. They both think you are a smart boy with a bright future. They asked us so many questions about you." She picks up her water and takes a big gulp, and then looks around.

I know what she's looking for, so I run into the dining room and grab a coaster from the buffet. I place it on the coffee table. "Here you go."

She places her glass on the table, reaches down, and takes off her shoes with both of her hands and places them under the chair. She curls her feet up next to her.

"Especially Dean. He said he did the X-rays but the results aren't in yet." She turns to my father. "Is that possible?" Without giving him a chance to answer, she turns back to me. "Anyway, he wanted to know so much about you and about us. I think he may want to offer you a job at his medical clinic or something. Why else would he ask so many questions?"

My stomach is turning. What's Dean trying to do? She'll eventually see through his questions and realize what he's trying to find out.

I look over at my dad. He's just sitting there listening to all of this as if he's hearing it for the first time as well. I know that face. That's the *I'm not going to commit to anything until your mother has finished speaking, then I will agree with everything she says* face. I look back at my mother, and without skipping a beat, she continues.

"The art school thing is a hobby. You are a man now. You don't need hobbies. You need to have a man's job and a man's responsibilities." Her face lights up. "Could you imagine working in a doctor's office? Wouldn't that be wonderful? We would be so proud." She turns toward my father. "Wouldn't we, Eli?"

"No job was officially offered."

"Don't be negative. Why else with all the questions about Evan?"

Maybe she's gotten away with it for so long that the idea someone would figure it out completely eludes her. I try to keep my voice steady. "Mom, what would I do at a doctor's office?"

"There is so much. You answer phones, work with patients, work on the computer, so much to do all day. Plus they would pay you good money and maybe even you can be a doctor." She is positively gleeful.

The fact that working at a doctor's office is not the way to *be* a doctor doesn't even factor into this conversation.

"What kind of questions were they asking about me?"

"Oh, I don't know. Just be glad someone of worth is taking an interest." She reaches for her glass of water. "Plus their lovely daughter Maria. Both are blessings for you from God."

"It's late, Voula. We should all go to bed and talk about this later." My dad gets up. "Evan, don't you have work tomorrow?"

"Yes, and Saturday."

My mother gets up and heads to the kitchen with her water glass. "We will see them on Sunday at church. More can be discussed then. Don't forget to pray tonight and thank God for giving you this gift." She pauses. Smiles. "Even though you don't deserve it."

It's Sunday morning, and today I get to drive to church in my own car. This is because my mother has still been high on the notion that I will be working in a doctor's office and eventually will marry the Greek doctor's daughter. It's also because my father made sure that my mom and I both understood that this was my Christmas present.

I get to come back home after church.

In my car.

By myself.

I'm in my room putting on my charcoal-gray suit when I hear my phone vibrate on the bedside table. It's Henry:

What ru doing?

Puttin on a suit 4church. U?

Just lying in bed wishing u were here. Send me a pic suitman!

I grab my tie and put it on. I adjust my suit jacket, open the closet door, and center myself in the mirror. I try to fix my hair, but it's really no use. I take a full-length picture of my reflection and send it off to Henry.

Holy handsome fuck! I lv u in a suit, he texts back.

I text back, **Where's my pic?**

He sends a picture. Not one that I can frame or show anyone. He's not wearing a suit. He's not wearing anything.

I text: **oh! Wow. Damn ur a prblm.**

I'm a good prblm 2have. Miss u.

Me2.

Even though it's been a few weeks since I've been to church because of work, nothing much has changed. The sermon is eerily the same week after week, just a slightly different version of how sinful and unworthy we all are.

After the service we go downstairs to the basement for refreshments, and then usually we get invited to someone's house for lunch. We then return to church for evening service and dinner at someone else's home. It's an all-day thing. On the days when we're the ones hosting someone at our house, it's a nonstop day of reckoning.

Today, after service, we all gather in the church basement. I'm standing at one of the three long folding tables that are covered in plastic tablecloths from end to end. They have a cartoon-looking fall-leaf motif on them and floating Jesus heads. It's kind of an awesome combination and one that I always marvel over—I mean, the fact that you can purchase this somewhere is amazing. During Christmas, the tablecloth is a floating baby Jesus with randomly arranged ornaments and holly in the background. This is the table with the junk food snacks, chips, candy, and cookies.

Maria Boutouris spots me and skips over. She's literally skipping.

"Hi, Evan."

"Hey. How are you?"

"I'm great. You look nice."

"Thank you?" That's uncomfortable. "Nice . . . bracelet," I say, trying to find something appropriate to comment on.

"Thanks. I made it. Are you coming over today?"

"I'm sorry?"

"Your family has been invited over to our house after we're done here."

"I have homework, so probably not."

I have never been happier to see our pastor. He says, "Evan, can we talk privately? Whenever you're done here with the lovely Miss Boutouris." He looks down and smiles at Maria.

I follow him to the office and sit across from him. He has his hands folded. He is smiling in a kind, distracted way. "How have you been?" His voice is serious.

"Okay, thanks. You, Pastor?"

"I'm fine, Evan. Dr. Boutouris said you were in a car accident?"

"Yes. Yes. Everything is okay now, though. I'm okay. . . ."

"Evan, he told me about what he saw. He's concerned. You know I already was. Am."

I nod.

"I haven't spoken to your parents. I should have before, but I somehow believed it would work itself out." He takes a short breath. "I was wrong. And I'm so sorry. I failed you." He pauses. "Also, I know about the video."

I swallow. "Pastor?"

"A lot of people have seen it, but I'm assuming your parents—"

"I don't think my mother has."

"Your father?"

"I think he may know."

"What about all the marks on your body?"

"I told the doctor about my clumsiness."

"He said the X-rays show a lot of damage. Not from the fight."

"Wow. Whatever happened to doctor-patient confidentiality?" I sound irritated, which I am. I don't like being ambushed, no matter how good the intentions are.

"He's concerned and so am I. This is more serious than I thought. I need to talk with your parents."

I don't say anything. I just sit there. Thinking.

"Evan, I know this is a personal matter."

"It is. It's very personal. Pastor, what do you think will happen when you talk to my parents?" I don't give him a chance to answer. "She'll stop? He'll all of sudden put an end to what she does? Take a stand, a side for once?" My voice is getting angrier, but not louder. "None of that will happen. It will only get worse."

"I understand how you feel."

"What? Please don't say that. It's so—condescending." And all of a sudden, it becomes clear to me. "You can't say anything, because you can't fix this. I'm the only person who can."

There's a knock on his office door. He says, "Yes?"

"Pastor, it's Voula. Voula Panos." The pastor and I look at each other. I nod.

"Come in, sister." He stands as she enters, all smiles.

"Praise God, Father." She looks at me. "Evan, honey. Are you okay?"

I raise my hand to signify that I'm fine.

The pastor says, "I just wanted to check in with Evan and see how he's doing."

"We continue to pray for him. Please don't stop, Father."

He nods.

"C'mon, Evan. The Boutouris family wants to see you before you have to go home to do homework." She links her arm through mine and walks me out of his office. As we're walking up the stairs she whispers, "What kind of lies are you telling the pastor?"

"I didn't tell him anything. But he knows." I feel a rush of energy. Maybe it's because everyone is trying to tell me what to do, or maybe it's because I'm less afraid of what will happen to me. Of what she can do.

"Knows what?"

"What you do to me. And the reason he knows is because it's in my journals. Which you gave him to read. Odd, right? You were the one. Not me. After all this time, *you* told your secrets. You disgraced yourself."

I don't bother to look at her for a reaction. I quickly walk out of the church, trembling, and make my way to the parking lot. It's cold outside, probably mid-thirties, but it actually feels good. Refreshing. I get in my car and start driving. I'm not sure where I'm headed, but I just need to drive somewhere I feel safe.

I end up at the monastery. Then I am on my knees on the ground, digging. It's always more difficult to dig up the box when the ground gets this cold. At least I'm not chipping at ice.

I lift out the whole metal box and carry it to the trunk of the Tercel. I go back to the tree and cover the hole with dirt so that no one will know I was here. Looking back at the monastery, I squint to see if I can make out the statues, but I can't.

I text Henry:

Do u want 2go 4drive?

He texts back:

Yes! Where ru?

At monastery. Coming over.

I can't get to Henry's fast enough. I want to see the faces of people who don't judge. I want to learn to believe they mean it.

I park outside his house and practically run up the porch steps. Before I even get a chance to ring the bell, the door swings open and Henry is standing there. I hug him. Hard. So hard that I can feel my ribs hurt, but I don't care.

"Evan?" Mrs. Kimball appears behind him.

"Hi, Mrs. Kimball. Thank you for the great dinner. It was awesome."

She comes over and hugs me for what seems like forever. When she pulls back, she takes a good look at my face. It's the first she's seen me since it happened. I'm in much better shape than I was, but there are still enough marks to make her shudder.

"You're a beautiful boy. They can't take that away." She puts one arm around me, and we move into the hallway. Henry closes the door behind us and follows. "You guys want something to eat?"

I turn around and look at Henry, and he says, "We're good, Mom. We're going to head out."

Claire waves from the family room and yells, "Hey, Fancy Suit. Were you at a funeral?"

"He was at church, Claire." This from her dad, who I can hear but can't see.

Claire starts walking toward the hallway. "How does your face feel? It doesn't look as bad as I thought it would. I mean, not that you look bad. But it doesn't . . . oh hell."

"It's fine. I'm okay."

Mrs. Kimball breaks the tension. "Evan, thank you for standing up for Henry. Things have been a bit . . . Not everyone is as understanding as we would have hoped."

"I didn't really. I mean, Henry is . . ." I look over at him. His eyes are blinking rapidly and his head is slightly down.

Mr. Kimball, from the family room: "We just want you to be safe."

Henry says, "It's okay, guys. We don't have to figure it all out right now." He turns to me. "We should go."

Usually, Henry is driving, but today I am.

The Tercel and I are leading the charge.

"Where are you taking me?" Henry feigns concern.

"Do I have to tell you?"

"I've never been kidnapped before. It's kind of exciting." He stares out the passenger window. After a moment, he goes, "Do you believe in God?"

"Um . . . I don't know." This is something I've thought about. A lot. "I'd like to believe that something is out there, bigger than us. We can't be *it*. . . . I just . . . I don't know what 'God' looks like."

"I think God is probably awesome and looks at all this stuff we say and do and shakes His head." Henry is still looking out the window. "Wait, are you getting on the freeway?" He turns to me, smiling. "Where are we going?"

I briefly glance at him and then I look back at the road. "Patience." In a moment I say, "I shouldn't believe in anything. Sometimes I don't. I used to pray for God to help me and that never happened, but maybe that's not the way it works."

"I know what I want to do would cause more pain and

trouble for you." Henry's voice sounds dark.

I look over at him briefly before turning my attention back to the highway. We sit in silence for a little longer because what do I say? *Thank you. Thank you for wanting to do that for me. Thank you for loving me.*

Henry goes, "Hey, you're taking me into the city."

"Maybe."

Lake Michigan opens out right in front of the Field Museum of Natural History. There's a small area by the lake where the water meets the jagged rocks. Not many people go to that spot, especially this time of year. It's cold and windy and not easy to get to or walk around in, but the view looking back onto the city of Chicago is breathtaking. You can see the shoreline and how it curves to meet these tall boxes that are lit up, bursting from the ground.

Henry and I sit on one of the jagged rocks and try not to get blown over. The wind is fast and constant. The collar of my suit jacket is turned up and I'm holding the jacket closed with my very cold hands. Henry's quilted coat is zippered all the way up. He catches his breath from the rushing wind.

"This is so incredible! Can you even hear me with this wind?" He laughs.

His hair is being whipped around and his squinty eyes look almost closed shut. Our cheeks are bright red. He rests his head on my shoulder and we sit like this for as long as we can stand it.

The sky is clear and a cool, gray color. The water's choppy

and hard, and has the hue of a charcoal pencil. I want to draw it, but I'm not sure I could do it justice. This view and all it includes is strong. It can take everything that gets thrown its way. No matter the harshness of the season, this sky, this water, these trees keep standing here, defying the elements.

I tell myself I belong to this view, this sky, this lake, these trees. *I belong here with him.*

thirty-eight

As I stand in my room, later that evening, it feels smaller than the last time I saw it. I used to like the way it felt like a cocoon, a shelter. But now, standing in the center of it, I feel too large for the space. I take out some loose paper from my top desk drawer and start a new sketch. It's the lakefront. The way it felt this afternoon.

I hear the front door unlock. I look at my phone. It's 9:07 p.m. I put the sketch away and walk out of my room.

"Are you ready for school tomorrow?" My dad is taking off his coat.

"I am." But I'm not looking at him. I'm looking at my mother.

She takes off her coat and hangs it in the hall closet and motions to my father to hand his over. She takes it and hangs his up next to hers. She runs her hands over her dress to smooth every crease and walks into the kitchen. "Elias, do you want some coffee?" She is ignoring me.

"Yes." My father looks at me and motions with his eyes for me to come sit with him in the dining room. I do.

My mother returns. She places one coffee mug on the table as well as the cream and sugar. Working as a waitress at my uncle's restaurant all those years has given her the skills to carry multiple plates and cups all at once without breaking them. She disappears back into the kitchen and comes back with the other mug.

My dad says to me, "How was your time with the Boutouris family?"

But then my mother is back. "Yes, what did you tell Dr. Boutouris?"

"I'm sorry?"

She adds cream and sugar to hers and slowly stirs. She doesn't take her eyes off the top of her coffee mug. "You know, you're an interesting character."

I stay silent.

"You can play the victim without even breaking a sweat. You plant seeds that grow into lies in order to sabotage us." Finally she looks directly at me with the slightest smile. "You have disgraced us."

My dad takes a sip of his coffee.

"Your father may be fooled or be soft to your evil, but I

am not. I am right with the Lord and He gives me strength." That last word is spoken so loudly that it even startles my dad. She returns to her singsong way of speaking. "You make people feel sorry for you. For you? If they knew the real you, they would beat you as well to rid you of your sin and your ugliness."

A long time ago I stopped thinking that I could be surprised by the adults around me. My whole childhood was spent being a literal and emotional punching bag. After a while, if you're lucky, you learn survival skills by going with the punch instead of against it. I'm not going to try to set the record straight because I was taught a long time ago what little to no use that is. But something in me is churning and burning, and one by one, I can feel all the emotions I've worked so hard to contain start to break free.

"You disgrace our family by telling strangers lies and then you go ahead and tell the whole school about your deviant seed inside you. You tell them?"

"Voula, no more."

"We have no son. We. Have. No. Child."

My right leg begins to shake.

My father looks back down at his coffee mug and clenches his jaw and then starts to speak. "I think we should all talk with the pastor. As a family."

Everything is in slow motion. What's odd is that, in this moment, right now, I feel nothing. Not sad, happy, mad, or anything. I am sitting there filled with peace when *bam!*

Her coffee mug slams into my face. All of a sudden the slow motion has sped up and now we're in fast forward. *Bam!* Now my dad is restraining her. She's screaming and trying to get away from him. He's holding her back and I can't hear or make out what she's saying. Everything goes back to slow motion. And then there's no sound.

She breaks away from his grip and lunges toward me, throwing me off the chair and onto the ground. I'm lying on my back as she straddles me and starts beating my chest and spitting in my face. My dad is trying to pull her off of me.

Then the silence breaks.

"I want you dead!"

He jumps up behind her again and tries to keep her down. She keeps screaming.

"I'd rather mourn a dead child than have you around." She flings both arms and loosens her grip from him. She grabs a wooden tray from the table and raises it above her head, bringing it down right toward my chest. I raise my arms to block it and they take the blow.

"There's a video. A. *Video.* Of you telling the whole world you're a *pousti*! We are ruined. Humiliated. You killed us. You don't even have the decency to tell us that happened. We have to find out from strangers." She is thrashing and trying to escape my father's grip.

"Voula. Voula! You have to stop."

"I've always hated you since you came out of me. All I wanted was a good family." Still being held by my father, she starts to weep. "I wanted a family that would take away my pain. My memories. A good place where everything is the way it should be." She's sobbing.

"Voula, this is a good family. I knew. I knew, do you hear me? I read some of the journals. I saw the video. I've known."

Suddenly, my dad looks eight feet tall.

All at once, she goes limp. She's still right above me. Looking right at me and now completely limp. He lets go of her hands. I'm lying on the floor totally still.

A moment passes. Her eyes light up again. Her hands turn to fists and now she begins to pummel him.

Maybe it's the anger I've stored up all these years, or maybe it's the sight of her beating someone else for a change. But it's like something has finally snapped.

I grab my mother with enough force to shake her off my father. I run with her into the wall of the dining room and slam her body up against it. I'm pinning her against the wall and staring right into her eyes. The thing that has control of my body now creeps into my brain. I can feel my dad behind me. He tries to get me off her the way he was trying to get her off me. I hold her with one hand and fling him away with the other.

I want to say something, but I have a feeling this thing will

300

be hijacking my voice as well. Maybe I am possessed after all.

"You can't hurt him. Stop. *Stop!*"

It's not my voice, but it is my voice.

I lift her away from the wall and shove her back into it again as a way to make a point. And there it is—she's angry and furious and her eyes are full of sadness and hate. But there's something else there. Fear.

I drop her, and all of a sudden it's gone. The thing that took over has left just as quickly as it arrived, leaving me standing there.

Evan Panos.

Just me.

My voice is calm and steady. "I'm gay. Mom. Did you hear me?"

I stare at my mother on the floor crying. I get down to where she is. She looks right at me and spits in my direction. It lands on my face. I wipe it away as I say, "I'm not evil. I'm not ugly. I'm not perfect. I'm a good person. A really good person." She continues to sob, and by this time I do as well. "I'm still that boy you came to pick up in Greece. Do you want me? The way I am?" I'm looking right at her.

"My God is disgusted with who you are." She stops. Looks at me, and for a moment I see her eyes soften. Then she says, "I am too."

My dad comes up behind me and swoops me up. He carries

me to my room. Puts me in bed. Kisses my forehead and shuts my door.

"Evan. Evan." My dad nudges me.

I look up at him. *Where am I?*

I look around. It's my room.

"Wake up. It's almost six a.m."

I get up. I'm still in my clothes. My whole body aches. I grab my hat, slip on my shoes, and walk outside to the car. I'm going through the motions. It's like I'm not even aware of what's happening, it's just happening out of habit. Routine. Everything's back to being in slow motion. Once in the passenger seat, I flip down the visor and look at my face in the mirror.

"I cleaned the cuts and put Band-Aids on the bad ones."

"Thanks." I look over and he's not smoking. You'd think this would be a good time to light up. I go back to gazing at my head in the small mirror. The Band-Aids are small, so the cuts can't be that big, but the bruise sure is. I can now feel my head, and it's throbbing.

"You don't have aspirin in here?" I rummage through the glove compartment.

"No." My dad pulls the car over.

"What. Where are we—"

"I'm sorry."

"Are we going to the . . ." I stop myself. I look at him. I've never seen my father cry. He's not crying now. He doesn't talk about feelings.

"She'll get past this. I promise." He's looking straight ahead.

"Dad. Please."

"I know her. She's always so sorry afterward. It's like something else takes over and she can't help it." He turns to me. "She loves you."

"I can't be loved like this anymore. It's going to kill me."

This is the closest I've seen him come to pleading with me. "I won't let that happen."

"Dad. You don't stop her. Really stop her."

"Listen. We'll go get doughnuts. We'll go for a drive. Give her time to relax and then we'll make a plan. See the pastor. Pray. With God's help we can do this."

"Dad. I'm going to move out." I can't believe I just said that. But I realize it's true. It's what I've been waiting for since I turned eighteen.

He looks back in front of him and I half expect him to fight me on it. But after what seems like an eternity, he nods. Just like that.

I continue. "Going back isn't—I don't know how to fit myself back into that box. Back to that world anymore. I couldn't do it even if I wanted to. I think I've . . ."

"I can help you move." His hands are firmly on the steering wheel, yet they're trembling. He takes a breath. "We can pack

your things when I get back. There may be a place you can . . ."
He stops and looks at me. He shakes his head. "Evan, my heart
is beating so hard and fast it feels like I have two."

I don't know what to say so I put my hand on his shoulder.
He starts to weep.

We pull into the Dunkin'. Once inside, my father waves at
Linda and motions for me to sit down. He speaks with her for
a minute alone. She looks my way and gives me a sweet smile.
He sits down next to me and we have our usual order in silence.
After we're finished he drives me back home and waits for me
to get in my car and drive away. He heads to work. I drive to
the monastery.

I'm parked outside the gate, the metal box in the passenger seat
next to me. I'm ripping out pages from the notebooks.

Flipping and ripping.

This page? *No.*

This? Yes.

Yes.

Yes.

No.

No.

Yes.

thirty-nine

I am in the school parking lot behind the wheel of my car when Jeremy knocks on the window. I jump about ten feet. I roll the window down and he goes, "Dude, whose car is this?"

I sigh. "Get in."

He comes around to the passenger side, opens the door, throws his backpack into the backseat, and drops into the seat next to me. "When did you get this?"

"It doesn't—"

"Panos, is your face—"

"Let's not."

"Who—"

I want to blow it off, but that's not what I'm doing anymore. "My mother. I'm not accident prone."

"Fuck. I don't—"

"You don't have to. Just sit here with me, okay? I'm waiting for Henry."

"Oh." He hangs his head a little. "He probably hates me."

"Yep. Blame him?"

"No."

We sit in silence before Jeremy says, "Can I go in with you guys?"

"It's probably not going to be good."

"I feel like an asshole." He squints toward the school. "You know, I don't totally get . . . what you and Henry are . . . but I know that what happened isn't right. You shouldn't get the shit beat out of you for who you are."

I look at Jeremy. "I'm gay. Henry too. That's it. Everything else is . . . well, it's all the same. Really." Jeremy nods.

We get out, and I think I can practically hear Jeremy breathing. He looks scared to death. His usually pink face is white. Paper white. Henry spots us and starts walking over.

"You've got to be kidding me."

I say, "He wants to come in with us."

Henry lifts my chin with his hand and starts to examine my face. I pull away. "Sorry. It's a little tender."

"Ev, this . . ."

"She can't hurt me anymore. This was the last time."

I look at Jeremy, who hasn't moved at all, then back at Henry. "He knows he fucked up."

Henry sighs. "It's your call."

"I guess I want him to come in with us too."

Henry looks at Jeremy and slightly changes his tone. "As

much as I want to punch your face right now, at least you're not a complete asshole."

I remember the first time I entered high school. The anticipation and anxiety of what this place would be was overwhelming. It looked so big and frightening that I was sure the best way to make it through would be to keep my head down and go unnoticed.

Okay, so that hasn't exactly played out.

The three of us are walking up to the entrance and part of me feels the same anxiety I felt that first day as a freshman, but now there's another feeling. One of belonging. I belong with these two people I'm walking with.

Once inside, we all look at one another, knowing that, at the very least, we're going to have stories to share at the end of the day.

"Your F-squad growing?"

That didn't take long. Tommy and his pals are wasting no time. I'm figuring the F in F-squad isn't referring to fun.

Ali chimes in. "Jeremy? Really? I guess it figures."

Before anyone can react, Principal Balderini appears and physically gets between them. He's not a fast man, but he is large. Over six foot two and built like a defensive lineman.

"Nope. This isn't going to happen." He's blocking them. "Everyone is going to class. Now."

People start to disperse. Mr. Balderini says, "Tommy,

Lonny, Scott, and Gabe. You stay close." He then zeroes in on me. He continues, "Everyone to class. We're all on high alert. No shenanigans." He stares right at Tommy with that one. "Mr. Panos, my office, please." He turns to Tommy and the others. "You all will wait outside my office. I'll be with you next."

This is the second time in my whole high school tenure that I've been to the principal's office. I sit across from Principal Balderini, waiting for some sort of lecture.

"Take a seat." He drops into his chair. "You're back now."

"Yes, sir."

"How was your week? Thanksgiving?"

"Fine."

"I had a conversation with Henry's parents. I've watched the video. Spoken with the others involved after viewing the video."

"Yes, sir."

"Mr. and Mrs. Kimball wanted to make a few things clear."

"Yes."

"Mr. Panos?"

"Yes, sir?"

"You didn't start it. I'm sorry." He shakes his head.

"I blacked out for some of it."

"It looks that way. The students involved will be dealt with. The video is with the police and they will need a statement from you."

He clears his throat. Stares down at his desk. When he looks up again, I can see the frustration and sadness, and for the first time I think, *What a hard job this must be.*

His voice is firm but soft as he says, "You can always speak to me. I want you to know that you will always have a safe place here. I'll make sure of that."

"Yes, sir."

"I'm sorry if I or anyone else here at this school has made you feel misunderstood or unsafe."

"Thank you." As much as I appreciate what's happening here, the guy can't even begin to comprehend the half of it.

I'm barely halfway down the hall before Tess Burgeon and two of her volleyball teammates pop up next to me.

"Hi, Evan." Tess seems to have more pep than usual. "Good holiday?"

"Sure. Yours?"

"Probably not as good as yours. Nice face, by the way." This from Leesha Johnson.

We're at my locker now and I turn around to look at all three of them. I've never had any kind of real, lasting experience with any of these girls. The only reason I've ever spoken to Tess was because I was hoping to help Jeremy, before . . . well, before everything.

"So—I feel a little better knowing that it had nothing to do with me when your boyfriend wasn't interested." I think that Tess is gloating. "He wouldn't have been interested in any girl."

I roll my eyes and turn to my locker. I can hear them walking away.

All but one.

"Come on, Kris!" Tess yells.

I turn around and see Kris just looking at me. She half smiles. "Good to have you back, Evan."

I smile back.

forty

Everybody says this, but this Christmas really did come out of nowhere. In the last few weeks here's what happened:

I lost my job at the deli, due to business slowing down.

I got that internship at the art gallery. My new small studio apartment is two towns over and allows for uninterrupted work on drawings. I even taped back together the drawings my mother had torn and stacked on my bed. I brought them back to life like Frankenstein's Monster and turned them in to Mr. Q.

And lastly, I now work at the Dunkin'. My shifts are all over the place and some of them are with Linda. Also, it turns out, I'm not sick of doughnuts. Yet.

On my early-morning shifts, I see my dad. It's weird to be on the other side of the counter waiting on him. Linda lives in the duplex in the front. My studio is in the back; it used to be storage, but it has a bathroom. I'm not sure if it's a legal rental, but it's a palace as far as I'm concerned. Linda stops by from time to time to make sure I'm eating. I get a lot of day-old doughnuts and bagels.

I see my dad about once a week. I haven't seen my mother since I left. I know it's going to sound odd, but I miss my family. Not my actual family, but the idea of what my family could have been. I wonder sometimes what would have happened, where we'd be, if just one thing were different—if somehow one of the bad things that took place never existed. Would that have made a difference? Would we still be together?

My phone buzzes.

When ru coming over?

I text back: **Leaving soon.**

Henry texts back: **Merry Xmas**

Henry is the first to greet me with a hug and peck on the cheek. His parents are great, but real kissing is still not something we're comfortable with in front of them. "Merry Christmas!"

"Merry Christmas." I hug him back.

Claire and Mr. Kimball are already at the kitchen island.

"Mom, you have to make more bacon. The rest of the family and Nate are not going have enough when they get here." Claire adds three more strips to her plate.

"Merry Christmas." Mrs. Kimball puts her arms around me.

"What time is everybody coming over again?" Henry asks.

"Just before dinner, like around fiveish?" Mr. Kimball comes over and hugs me with one arm.

"Evan and I are going to go for a drive. It's really clear out there today."

We are?

I look at him, a little perplexed. He raises his eyebrows at me and grabs a single pancake from the stack. "Let's go!"

In Henry's car I resist the urge to ask where we're going. Instead I say, as casually as I can, "This is my first Christmas with your whole family."

"Feeling the pressure?" He looks over at me. His hair is extra floppy today.

That's a problem. I sit on my hands.

"Nervous?" he asks.

"Of course."

"You should be. I'm kinda the golden child. The expectation is high."

"Claire is the golden child. You're a child."

We both laugh.

"It'll be great, and whatever isn't, we'll make great. Honestly, there are only two idiots in our family and even they won't say anything. If they do, you know Claire will shut that shit down." He reaches for my hand.

We're parked as close as we can by the rocks that meet the lake, right below the Field Museum. We sit there with the car running and look at the skyline.

"It's magic, right?" I can hear the awe in Henry's voice.

"Yep."

He turns to me and smiles a soft, even smile. Maybe it's the sun reflecting off the frozen lake and bouncing in through the windshield, but his green eyes look bigger and brighter than I've ever seen them.

He takes my left hand in his right and our fingers grab on so tightly they begin to feel numb. But this kind of numb is the good kind. The last thing I want is for this moment to end, but I made a promise to Mr. Kimball. "We should get back before it gets too late."

"Stay here a minute. I have to get something."

He climbs out of the car, and the cold air comes in like a blast. He jogs to the trunk, and I can see him in the side mirror. He's pulling something out, but I can't make out what it is. The door opens again, and the cold comes back in with Henry. He sinks into the driver's seat and hands me a package wrapped in brown paper. It's rectangular and about the size of a shirt box.

I say, "My gift for you is back at the house. I thought we were all doing presents tonight. With your family."

"This is for you. I didn't want to give it to you with anyone else around."

The light shining into the car is casting this glow on Henry's face. Every feature looks like it's sculpted from perfect, flawless stone, except that he's real.

My hands are shaking. I run my fingers over where he's

written EVAN on the top right-hand corner of the package. Just to make sure it's really there. I turn it over and slowly tear at the seam.

Inside is a brown cardboard box. I flip the box, place it on my lap, and lift the lid.

I look back up at Henry. His eyes are wet.

I look back down at the box. I peel away the white tissue paper. Inside are ten black and white composition notebooks. Each one has a title box in the center with a few wide-ruled lines.

On each book cover, in the title box, he's written: *For Every Normal Day.*

I feel the tears come rushing down. "You remembered."

He nods. Softly he says, "It's a start."

And then he reaches for me and pulls me to him.

Author's Note

"If you want to be loved, never show people who you truly are."

I first heard those words from my family when I was five years old. They would be repeated often and have haunted me for most of my life. I believed and lived by them. Eventually I grew to hate what they stood for.

In this book, Evan is terrified about being found out. About the abuse at home and about his sexuality. As many of us do, he tries hard to compartmentalize the different pieces of his life to cope. But eventually, he can't do it any longer, and all the pieces come to light.

In my own life I spent many years trying to hide like Evan. I grew up in a small midwestern town in a strict Greek household, and I was terrified of being found out. Would being "found out" make my family love me less? Would I lose the few friends I had worked so hard to make in high school?

When my family and I arrived in America, like most immigrant children, I had one goal: to fit in. To try to be a part of this new world. Standing out was never a goal, but it was almost impossible not to. I didn't look like all the other kids in our small town. My home-packed school lunches smelled weird. I barely understood this new language, and when I did eventually speak it, it was with an odd, stuttering accent. There were unexplained bruises on my face and body. And I was gay.

All this added up to a portrait of someone who wasn't doing a great job blending in. But I tried, working hard at being a good student, a good Christian, a good son. I failed miserably at all of it, until I no longer could fake it. I no longer wanted to. My own personal coming out was slow, over time, and not as bold as Evan's. I struggled with accepting myself, but once I did, my life took on real meaning.

Even though I had been encouraged by therapists to write down my experiences as a way of healing, I could never get beyond the first page. It was too painful. I had gotten to a place where I could talk to a professional, but putting it down on paper felt too revealing, too raw.

My best friend, Jennifer Niven, suggested I give the story to someone else. That night I started writing and Evan suddenly appeared.

I've been incredibly fortunate in the way my life has unfolded over the years, but that hasn't happened by accident. There have been a number of amazing people who have shown me the true meaning of unconditional love and support. People who have become my chosen family.

Feeling isolated, afraid, suicidal, wrong, and unworthy are all things I have wrestled with. Thankfully, I learned that I'm not alone. I know there are many kids out there who are struggling—I've met them when I've traveled across the country for my work. Please know that there are people and organizations that are there to support you. They want to help. Let them. Reach out and show the world who you truly are.

LGBTQ ORGANIZATIONS

The Trevor Project—www.thetrevorproject.org

It Gets Better Project—www.itgetsbetter.org

LGBT National Help Center—www.glbthotline.org

GLSEN (Gay, Lesbian & Straight Education Alliance)—
    www.glsen.org

PFLAG (Parents and Friends of Lesbians and Gays)—
    www.pflag.org

ABUSE

National Child Abuse Hotline 1-800-4-A-CHILD
    (1-800-422-4453) and its affiliate,
    Childhelp—www.childhelp.org

BULLYING

Stomp Out Bullying—www.stompoutbullying.org

StopBullying—www.stopbullying.gov

Acknowledgments

When I lived in NYC, I walked every day for at least eight miles. A lot can be worked through on a great walk. Even more can be discovered, not just in the physical world around you but also in the one in your head. When I started writing *The Dangerous Art of Blending In*, I often would drift off to those NYC walks in my head. They held a lot of memories of personal experiences I was working out. When I finally finished putting them into a story, it was frightening to think that someone else might actually read them. That someone was my strong, smart champion of an agent, Kerry Sparks. Her wisdom, care, and editor's sensibility gave me the courage to write from a very authentic place. Thank you, Kerry, and everyone at Levine Greenberg Rostan for being such incredible champions.

Thank you, Alessandra Balzer, my genius editor at Balzer + Bray. Without your insight, intelligence, and complete confidence in this story, I'm not sure that I would have had the courage to dig deeper. Thank you for "having my back" and for being a fellow lover of meats and cheeses. Alessandra, you and the entire team at Balzer + Bray/HarperCollins make me look good: Kelsey Murphy, Renée Cafiero, Alison Donalty and Michelle Cunningham, Jenny Sheridan, Kathy Faber, Jessie Elliot, Kerry Moynagh, and Andrea Pappenheimer, Cindy Hamilton and Stephanie Boyar, Nellie Kurtzman, Sabrina Abballe, Bess Braswell, and Jace Molan.

Thank you to all my family of friends who never judge, always champion, and are more than ready to find the next great hole in the wall for food and beverages. Especially the immensely gifted and gorgeous Jennifer Niven, who listened to every far-flung idea and gently nudged me to be better. You, dear friend, my sister, my best, will never fully know what you mean to me.

Thank you to Judy Kessler for feeding me *the* best pasta dinners in Los Angeles. Ever. And for believing and seeing something in me all those years ago when I couldn't see it myself.

Thank you to one of my first readers, Beth Kujawski, for your wise words on a very rough initial manuscript and for all your baking genius. Seriously, what this woman can do with flour, butter, and sugar is nothing short of a miracle.

Thank you, Josh Flores, for being my first teen reader and for your contagious enthusiasm, not only for this story but for books and authors in general. I cannot wait to read your first book.

My dog Baxter, who sadly passed away six months before

this book came out, was a grumpy rescue who rescued me. For anyone who has a pet, you know all too well the power they have over our souls. Thank you, Baxter, for making it not easy but always worth it.

A big thanks most of all to Ed Baran (and his family) for taking such good care of my heart and always making sure that I knew how much I was loved. Such unconditional support and love has made so much possible, including this book.

Lastly, thanks to the number of people I spoke to who have thrived on the other side of childhood trauma. You are all my heroes.

Angelo Surmelis was raised in Greece until he immigrated to Illinois at the age of five. He currently lives in Los Angeles. An award-winning designer, Surmelis has been featured on over fifty television shows, including the *Today* show and *Extra*, as well as in magazines such as *InStyle*, *TV Guide*, and *Entertainment Weekly*. He has worked as a host on networks like HGTV and TLC. This is his debut novel. He can be found online here: www.angelohome.com.